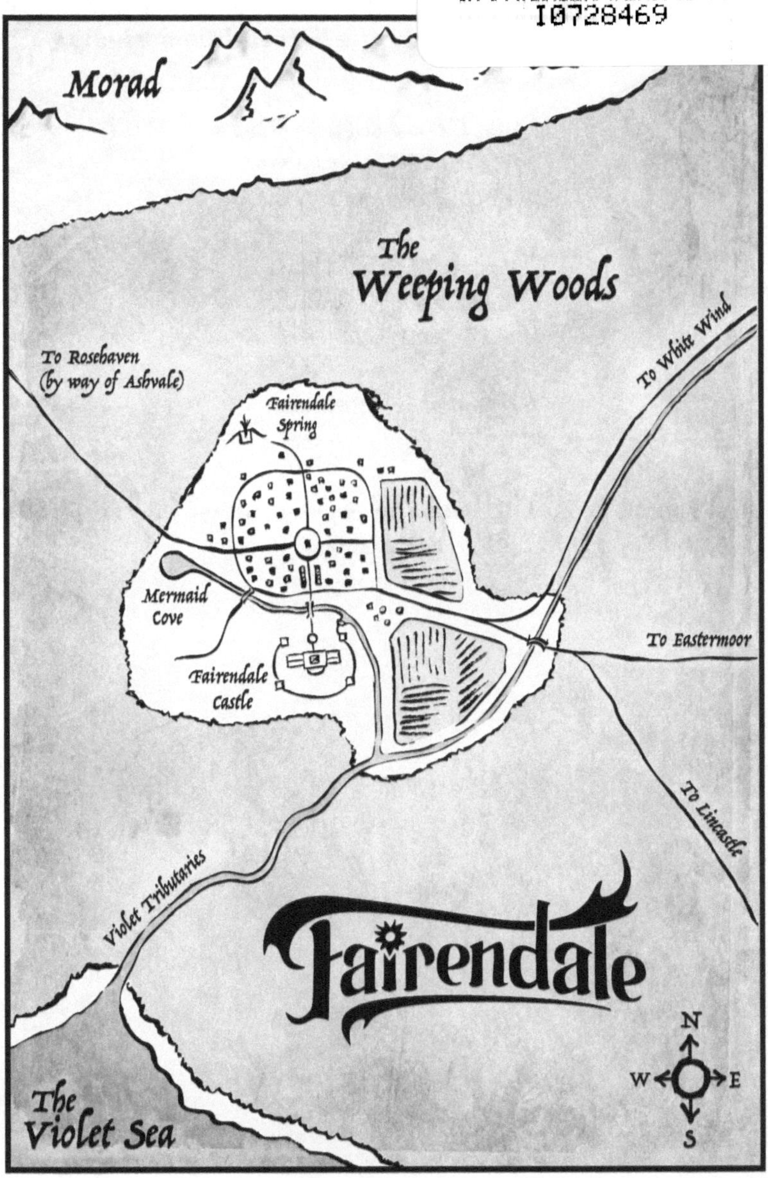

Morad
The Weeping Woods
To Rosehaven
(by way of Ashvale)
To White Wind
Fairendale Spring
Mermaid Cove
Fairendale Castle
To Eastermoor
To Lincastle
Violet Tributaries
Fairendale
The Violet Sea
N
W E
S

Read all the books in the Fairendale series!

Book .5: *The Good King's Fall (a prequel)*
Book 1: *The Treacherous Secret*
Book 2: *The King's Pursuit*
Book 3: *The Perilous Crossing*
Book 4: *The Dragons of Morad*
Book 5: *The Fiery Aftermath*
Book 6: *The Mysterious Separation*

Collector's Editions:
Books 1-6: *The Flight of the Magical Children*

To see all the books L.R. Patton has written, please click or visit the link below:
www.lrpatton.com/store

Fairendale

2

THE KING'S
PURSUIT

Batlee Press
PO Box 591596
San Antonio, TX 78259

First Edition—2016/Cover designed by Toalson Marketing
www.toalsonmarketing.com

L.R. PATTON

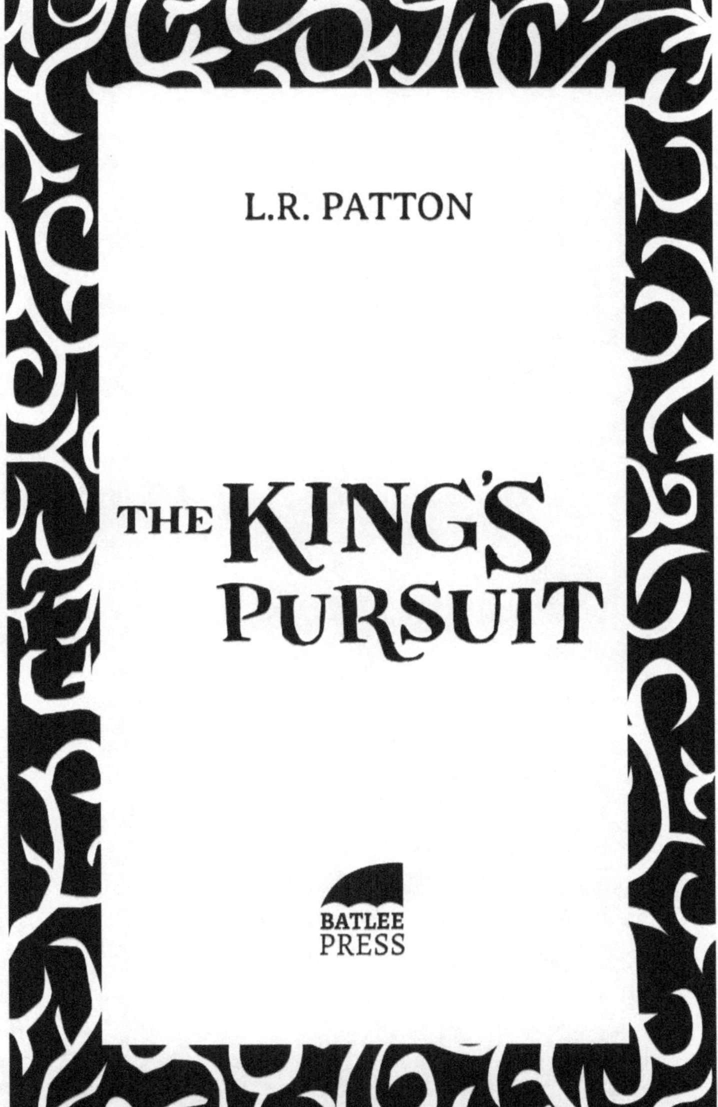

BATLEE PRESS

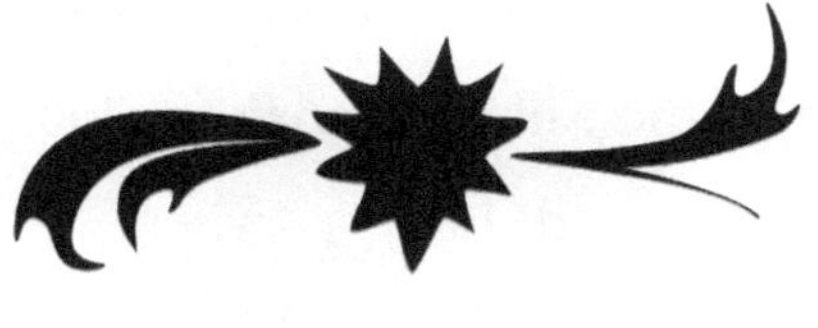

Move

The sun does not shine. It has simply disappeared in all the days after the children fled the village of Fairendale, some of them captured by the king of the land, some of them disappearing into the Weeping Woods that surround the kingdom, others gone missing entirely. Or perhaps the sun cannot find a reason to shine, for there is no longer laughter filling the streets of the village. There is only rain falling, pooling, washing away the red that the king's steward could not reach. The world has turned gray and cold.

Some of the people take to their beds, sick with grief over the loss of their children after King Willis decreed that every Fairendale child would be brought to his castle so he could find the magical one who might threaten his throne. The Roundup has stolen their children and their very lives, though these remaining villagers, in truth, go on living. There is a tragic difference, dear reader, between living as if one were dead and truly living.

This time, when Death moves through the streets, he does not glide in the same manner he does when there is fever and sickness and hunger, when he can steal his victims in one fell swoop. This is Heart Sickness, and it is a hold-on sort of dying, a slow dying, another every day, and so he waits. And waits. And waits.

Death does not like waiting.

But there is one who does not take to her bed. There is one who sits alone at her table where a daughter with green eyes used to sit. There is one who gazes out the window and watches the rain and ponders.

She ponders and ponders and ponders. She makes her plans.

And then, when the sky remains unchanged and she is sure the people will go on in their slow dying way, she moves.

For she was always a woman who moved.

The king paces on his pedestal, lumbering and slow. He

is a large man, one given to sweet rolls and sitting, and because he is royalty, neither is denied him. The court fills with men, but they do not make as much sound as one might expect from so much armor clashing against itself. King Willis watches them, impressed by the silence of their movements, mesmerized by the silver catching light, blinking at him. He would never tell them they impress him, of course, for then they would demand more provisions, and he is not a generous man, not anymore. Perhaps he was once upon a time, but a kingdom demands much of its king. A king cannot always remain generous.

King Willis watches his king's guard, and he swells with something akin to hope. This will be a good day. He is certain of it. These men will bring him news he wants to hear. News of found children.

King Willis nods at Sir Greyson, bidding him speak.

The king's son, Prince Virgil, stands beside him. It is time he became a king, King Willis has taken to saying of late. For when the lost children are found, when the one lost who holds danger over the throne is found, it will be Prince Virgil who will decide what must be done with him.

One might agree that our prince is too young for this sort of responsibility. And it is true that Prince Virgil does not like thinking about what might happen, about what he might have to do. So when his father's men come filing into the throne room, it is with different hopes that he watches them. Hopes that dare to say, *Keep them hidden. Keep them safe.*

"They are a sight," King Willis says. He stands beside his son now, one hand on Prince Virgil's shoulder. Prince Virgil tries not to notice his father's foul breath of garlic and lamb.

King Willis, in truth, places his hand on his son's shoulder not as a fatherly gesture but because his legs are buckling at the knees. He will need to sit down soon. He is out of breath, and his feet burn in their black boots. He hopes the men are nearly finished filing in. It is the king's custom, you see, to stand when his captain brings in the guard, but he did not know there were so many. Hundreds, but thousands? Are there thousands in this room? He cannot tell. Next time he will request a private meeting with the captain.

Prince Virgil says nothing. He merely stares, for the king's guard is quite a sight, even to a boy of twelve. They are clad in their sturdy metal breastplates and helmets that obscure their faces so they all look the same, but for their heights and muscular builds. Their swords, strapped across their waists, bump against their hips. They are a force.

"Think of it," King Willis says. "Just think of it." He

laughs, a silent laugh that ripples all the way across the room, collides with a wall, and careens back toward Prince Virgil. The prince is not entirely sure what is funny; he does not laugh along with his father but merely stares at the collection of men gathering in the room.

"Think of it," the king says again.

Prince Virgil also does not know what it is King Willis would like him to think of.

The king answers his son's silent question. "They are all yours."

Prince Virgil feels a jolt of something—fear? Pleasure? Thirst for this kind of power? He does not know that it is all three. That he could lead an army of men like this someday. That they would follow his every command.

That it might be stolen from him, when it is his, rightfully his.

Is it rightfully his without the gift of magic?

No.

Yes, of course it is.

The throne belongs to his family. His grandfather, the great King Sebastien, fought for it. He deserves to keep it. He will keep it.

But they are his friends. The children who live in the secret dungeon beneath the dungeon are his friends. The children who have gone missing are his friends. Surely a friendship is more valuable to our prince than a throne.

Alas, the hearts of men are not easy to understand.

The throne room grows quiet, dead still. The hall behind it ceases its shaking. The men have finally finished their entrance.

The king folds into his chair. It is the only way he can fit into it, this folding. He waits in the silence for one minute. Two. More. Prince Virgil shifts, but the soldiers remain perfectly, impressively still.

Finally, King Willis spreads his hands and says, in a booming voice that knocks against their armor: "Soldiers of the kingdom," and the men salute, one great, thundering clap. Prince Virgil jumps. His father smiles.

"Think of it," he says to his son. And this time Prince Virgil nods his head and smiles like his father.

"At ease," the captain, a man named Sir Greyson, tells his men. The men fall back but stand ordered, tall, frozen.

"Soldiers of the kingdom," King Willis says.

Only the captain moves. He removes his headpiece and bows to his king. King Willis waits until he rises again before continuing.

"For seven days you have traveled long and far and deep," King Willis says. He does not move from his seat on the throne. In truth, our king cannot move. His feet cannot support him any longer; they are much too tired, and they pulse their anger at him. And so he sits.

One might think that a man who sits cannot command as much power as a man who stands. But one has never met King Willis. A man so large, sitting or standing, could command a world of power.

King Willis is a man who loves his own voice, and though his feet find no relief in the sitting, though his back screams its ache, though his breath is short and hard, he will not lose any words in the speaking.

"You have been looking for thirty missing children," he says.

Garth, the king's page, raises a finger, clearing his throat. He is a tall boy with messy hair the color of Cook's milk-less tea. He stands straight, rigid, so as to appear more than a boy, but one look at his face tells otherwise. Fortunately, the king has not looked at his face in all these days after, or Garth might find himself trapped in the dungeons beneath the dungeons, with all the other children, some of whom could be his brothers and sisters. They have disappeared, you see, and Garth just this morning was handed by the kingdom's messenger another frantic letter from his mother. He has urged her to stop writing him at the castle, since he returns home every eve, but she is a mother who has lost eleven children. I am sure we could understand her grief. His mother wants to know where her children are. Garth wants to remain outside the dungeons. He does not have the gift of magic, but King Willis cares naught about gifts. He cares only for rounding up the children, all the children, for that is the only way he believes his kingdom will be safe from the one who would dare steal it.

The boy is terrified to interrupt, but he is more terrified of what might happen if the king were to miscount the missing children. The king glances at him for only a moment, hardly seeing him. Garth tries not to wither. The king has been known to run through pages like a book one might read, though he is a different kind of page. A Garth kind of page is a person employed to do whatever the king bids—run errands and open doors and help a king in and out of his golden chair, which is quite a large task. A page must also correct a king in his error, should he be brave enough. Garth, in truth, does much more than this. He also shines the king's shoes and keeps his plate filled and helps the king dress, though the king is fast running out of clothes that fit. He fears that he will not be able to perform this task someday soon. And what will happen then? Garth needs this job at the castle, for his family is very, very poor, and they need the food his coin buys them. Filling the bellies of eight boys and four girls in one village house is more than his poor mother can do, though now his brothers and sisters have disappeared, so it has become easier, in a way, though Garth's mother would not agree, for financial ease is never worth the life of a child. Garth does not know if his brothers and sisters sit in the dungeons or if they escaped from the king's men. He does not know where the dungeons lie. But he will. He is already searching.

"Yes, what is it?" the king says, clearly annoyed at the interruption. He is hungry again, and ready for this meeting to reach its end. His feet, though he is no longer standing on them, ache in a great pulsing clench. He will have to request a more comfortable pair of shoes. His are too unbearable, pinching at the toes and cutting into his heels.

"Thirty-one children, sire," Garth says. He does not stutter as he does on occasion, when fear grabs the words and keeps them lodged in his throat. He is surprised at his clarity. His eyebrows raise of their own accord.

The king waves his hand, as if dismissing his page. "Yes, very well," the king says. He takes a deep breath.

Now he must begin again, for this is what a king such as ours does when his eminent speech has met interruption. "Soldiers of the kingdom," he says. The commander bows and rises again. "For seven days you have traveled long and far and deep."

The men remain perfectly still. It is impressive to see, reader. Can you imagine it? Thousands of steel-clad men, with no eyes to see, for their headpieces obscure much of their vision (one might ask why soldiers would wear a headpiece like this one. Well, would you want your head exposed in battle?), all standing perfectly still. The sun reaches through one of the windows and catches the breast plate of one of the men. It locks eyes with Prince Virgil. He squints. Garth stares at the ray that appears to hold all the shapes in the world.

"You have been looking for..." A pause, a sideways look at Garth, who straightens and colors. "Thirty-one children. Tell me, what news do you bring us?"

If we were to turn our attention to the commander of the king's guard, we would know nothing of what he thinks or feels or what news he brings by studying his face. Sir Greyson has not flinched. He has not buckled. He has not moved at all. It would be difficult work to read the news that our good Captain Greyson brings his king. This is, of course, the very question Sir Greyson has dreaded the entire ride in this morning. He risks his life in his answer, as we shall soon see.

Sir Greyson clears his throat. "With respect, Your Highness," he says. He bows again. The king, however, is impatient.

"Yes, yes," King Willis says. His eyes gleam, as if waiting for good news, although a smarter man might deduce that no children brought in with the entire king's army means that no children have, in fact, been found. But King Willis is not a man for much thinking.

Prince Virgil has noticed. Even now, he looks from his father to the captain. Even now he wonders what might happen to this good man he has known all his life.

"We have been as far as the lands of Guardia in the north and to the very banks of the Violet Sea in the south. We have walked as close to the lands of Morad as we dared, and we have searched the wastelands of Ashvale in the west." He clears his throat again. "We have found nothing."

"You have found nothing?" the king bellows. "The children have all disappeared? Impossible!" The king struggles from his throne. Prince Virgil stares straight ahead, trying to ignore the page who rushes to his father's side, struggling, too, to pull the king from his chair.

No one else breathes. No one else moves. It is anyone's guess what will happen next. Prince Virgil hopes Sir Greyson will not suffer. His father could deem him incompetent. He could send him to the dungeons, or the dungeons beneath the dungeons. He could sentence him to death.

The same fears swirl and falter in Sir Greyson's mind, too. He has done what he could, but would the king believe it was enough? Would he throw something? Would he demand heads? Would he dismiss, or reassign, or toss them all, every last one of them, into the dungeons? Surely not. Surely he understands what this search has cost Sir Greyson's men, seven days and seven nights without rest and proper food and the presence of their families. Surely he will let them return home, at least for a time.

"They are hiding," King Willis says. When Garth finally pulls him from his chair, the king paces the stage before his guard. His steps thunder, shaking the pedestal that was built for him years ago. It trembles against the marble floor. King Willis is a man who prefers looking down on his people. Arthur, the village's most skilled furniture maker, was the man who crafted the pedestal. It is ornate, as is everything that Arthur has made, with swirls and flourishes and the kingdom crest, the head of a ferocious looking bear. Prince Virgil thought it magnificent and had told Arthur so on one visit to the village. King Willis hardly noticed it.

Sir Greyson's head hangs low now. "We have searched everywhere," he says.

"And you have questioned all the other kingdom people?" King Willis says.

"Yes, sire," Sir Greyson says. Even his voice is weary. His face has lines it never wore before this seven-day journey began.

"How is it you have come home so quickly?" King Willis says, as if he has only just now noticed that seven days was not nearly enough to travel the realm of seven kingdoms.

Sir Greyson gestures to the men behind him. "I sent out parties," he says. "The searching was urgent. We wished to find them before they reached the Violet Sea."

"As if children would travel the Violet Sea," King Willis says.

"We thought it worth pursuing," Sir Greyson says.

"And these men," King Willis says, as if "these men" are not in the very room where all gather. "They are trustworthy?"

Sir Greyson looks around at his men. He cannot tell who is who, for they all wear the same armor, none more decorative than another, but he knows them all by name. This is what makes Sir Greyson a great leader. He knows the names of his men. He knows their families. He knows their habits and which ones prefer falling asleep after a hand of cards and who prefers to eat their supper and retire early. He knows which ones have wives and how many children they have and what sorts of stories they enjoy telling the most. He is a commander who cares. And they are men he can trust.

"Yes, sire," he says. "I trust my men implicitly."

King Willis blows out a breath. He looks at the king's guard standing before him. He looks at Sir Greyson.

"No one has seen them, Your Majesty," Sir Greyson says.

"No one has seen them," King Willis says. He adds a laugh to the end of it, though it is not a laugh that carries merriment. "They are being given asylum."

Asylum, dear reader, is protection offered to one on the run.

"Perhaps," Sir Greyson says. "Perhaps they are. We questioned everyone in each kingdom."

"As far as Guardia," King Willis says. "Do you believe

the children of Fairendale could have traveled so far as all that in so little time?"

"With help, perhaps," Sir Greyson says.

"And who, I ask, might help children such as these?" King Willis says, though it is, perhaps, quite a silly question. Many people would help children in danger.

Sir Greyson does not answer such a silly question. He merely waits for the king to speak again. He is thinking, this moment, of the itch crawling around his beard. He longs to scratch it, but he is a disciplined man, and he has disciplined men to lead. What would his men think of their captain if they were expected to remain perfectly still in the presence of their king when he, their leader, took even a moment to scratch a persistent itch? That would not be authority. It would not be integrity. It would not be honor.

A leader who demands something of his men must be ready to sacrifice the same. This is precisely why Sir Greyson has never married, truth be told. When one says the vows to become a king's guard, there is a clause that says a man must be ready to forsake his family for the good of the kingdom. Sir Greyson does not know if he could do what some of his men have done. He does not know if he could round up children who were his. And, aside from all that, no one in the village seemed the least bit interested in the captain of the guard. There had been a woman once, but it was so long ago Sir Greyson could hardly remember what it was like being loved. He saw her every now and again, breezing about the village, her fiery hair gripping the wind as it had the day they had parted. He has not seen her since the roundup, the day her daughter disappeared.

"You," King Willis says. Sir Greyson flinches, as if woken from a sleep. He is exhausted from his travels, you see. That is the reason his attention wanders. "Must search them all again."

Sir Greyson does not say anything for a breath. Two. Three. Fifteen. And then he says, "If I may," which, in the kingdom of Fairendale, is like a code of sorts. Code for "I would like to speak candidly, please."

"Very well," King Willis says.

"I fear that some will question the peace between our kingdoms if we travel to our neighbors again," Sir Greyson says. "A second questioning could very well tell them we do not trust them."

King Willis waves his hand, dismissing this observation of Sir Greyson's, as if it is merely a small concern, though Sir Greyson knows better. The relations between the kingdoms and Fairendale have been tenuous since King Sebastien took all their men and killed them in a battle that benefited only him. The women and children left in the other kingdoms, at the time, could do nothing against King Sebastien's magic. The Great Battle is a story every child in Fairendale is told, and one cannot always know whether a story is true. But what if it is? What if the kingdoms, which bear men once more, should attack Fairendale tomorrow because of King Sebastien's cruelty all those years ago? King Willis does not have magic, and Prince Virgil is only a boy without magic. No one knows that, of course. Sir Greyson is not, in fact, supposed to know it.

They do not want war, do they?

"We do not trust the other kingdoms," King Willis says. "Interrogate them again."

Sir Greyson clears his throat, as if about to speak again, but King Willis turns an eye his way. His look is dark and challenging. Sir Greyson straightens his back.

Will he be able to do this for the king, knowing what might happen?

Of course he will. Sir Greyson is a man of duty, after all. He will do as his king commands.

"As you wish, sire," Sir Greyson says.

"Question every man, woman and child you find in all the kingdoms of the realm," King Willis says. "Search their houses and their woods and their wastelands. The children could be hiding anywhere. They must be found.”

“We shall begin with home,” Sir Greyson says. His men need and deserve a break. And they had not yet questioned the people of Fairendale, for the people’s wounds were too raw when the soldiers rode away on horseback. They had lost their children. They had lost friends as well. He does not hold any illusions that the people will be more helpful now than they were then. But at least his men will have tried. At least they will be home.

“The farthest lands,” King Willis says. “You shall start with the farthest lands.”

“We have not searched our own lands as thoroughly as we searched the distant ones,” Sir Greyson says. “The best place to hide is here.”

He does not know if this is what the children have done, of course, but he does know that his men will not be traveling for seven days and seven nights without rest yet again. There will be a mutiny, at best.

King Willis stares at Sir Greyson for a time. And then he smiles, a small, delighted smile. “Yes,” he says. “Yes, you are correct. You will search every inch of Fairendale and the Weeping Woods. That is where they shall be found. I am sure of it.”

“Yes, Your Majesty,” Sir Greyson says. His head dips in

a half-bow.

"They shall be found!" King Willis roars.

The guard, then, erupts, as is expected when a king gives what sounds like a battle cry, as this one does. Sir Greyson nods to the man on the end, and they begin their filing out in neat, clean lines. Sir Greyson stands tall until the last man has left the hall. Then he bows to his king, his face to the scarlet rug that travels the length of the room.

"That is all," King Willis says. Sir Greyson marches out.

When he is gone, King Willis shifts in his golden chair, attempting to find a position more comfortable than the one he assumed when his guard stood before him. Prince Virgil clears his throat and keeps his eyes on his father's face.

"I had almost forgotten you were here," King Willis says. Prince Virgil tries not to feel hurt at these words.

Garth holds a glass of water for King Willis. The king snatches it from the boy and drinks a long gulp and then hands the half-empty cup back to Garth.

"Some sweet rolls for the prince and me," the king says. Garth scurries out to do his bidding, not wanting, perhaps, to stay a minute longer in the room that smells like sweaty men who have not bathed in a week. Prince Virgil would like to go, too, but he cannot. His father has just ordered sweet rolls for him, which means the king would like his son to stay.

As it so happens, Prince Virgil loves sweet rolls. He is never one to pass up an opportunity to eat one or several. Sweet rolls, in the kingdom of Fairendale, are much like what I believe you call donuts in your kingdom. They are fried morsels of bread resembling a target with the bulls-eye cut out, covered in a sugary frosting that dissolves in one's mouth. Prince Virgil, I suspect, likes them as much as any child today likes a donut on occasion. Not all the time, of course. Sweet rolls are known to steal teeth.

So Prince Virgil waits, and while he waits, the king talks. He talks long, with waving arms and wiggling eyebrows, but after a time, Prince Virgil merely ceases to listen, hearing, instead, a drone such as what a bee might make if right beside one's ear.

"Well, son?" the king says, at long last.

Prince Virgil has just been wondering how long it takes for Cook to make sweet rolls. He has not heard what his father asked him. He stares at his father, trying to work his way back to the words at the beginning. His father said the children could be hiding in other kingdoms, but it was far more likely that they were hiding in the woods. That was the last clear thing Prince Virgil heard. And so he says, "Yes, father," somewhat woodenly.

"I will send out a decree then," King Willis says. "The prince has approved."

Prince Virgil feels a lurch in his stomach. What exactly is it he has approved? The death of the village children? He does not remember his father mentioning a decree. It must have been buried in all the words that buzzed about in his ears and then flew right back out.

"A decree," Prince Virgil says, hoping that his father will repeat himself, as he so often does.

"Yes," King Willis says. "Yes, I think it will work. A decree to the other kingdoms." King Willis stares off in the distance. Prince Virgil watches his father's mouth moving, but no sound comes out for a moment. Then King Willis says, "Something like, if any child has entered your kingdom in the last two weeks—perhaps a month, to be safe—you must send them back to Fairendale. They are fugitives, not innocents." The king's dark eyes lose their marble look. He turns to his son. "Meanwhile, our men can search closer to home."

Prince Willis does not ask how his father could command other kingdoms to do any of what he bids them, for he does not want to know, in truth. A stinging relief clots in his eyes. At least he has not unknowingly killed someone. At least the children are still safe. At least his friends…

Where are the sweet rolls? When can he leave this smelly room? He would like to sit on his balcony, in the open air, away from his father, please. "It is a good idea, Father," he says, as if his agreement might pass the time faster.

"You show good judgement, my son," King Willis says, though Prince Virgil is unsure how he shows good judgement by merely agreeing with his father. King Willis, you see, believes that good judgement means agreeing with those in charge. And because he is the one in charge, that, of course, means agreeing with his plans. We know that agreeing with another is not always the mark of good judgment. Good judgment is more than agreement. But that is not a lesson easily taught, especially not for one such as King Willis.

Prince Virgil nods his head, wishing those sweet rolls would come, and Garth walks in, carrying a plate heaped with them, two more empty plates tucked beneath his arm.

"Two for the boy," King Willis says.

Prince Virgil is slightly disappointed. There must be at least a dozen on the tray. Why can he not have more?

"We must not rot your teeth," King Willis says. He takes a great, massive bite of one that does not resemble a target with the hole cut out, for this one has cherry filling in its middle. The filling drips down his chin, but he does not seem to notice. Garth wipes it away, and King Willis finishes six sweet rolls before Prince Virgil has finished his two. When he is done, when there has been no other talking for several minutes, Prince Virgil takes leave of his father.

"Good-bye, father," he says.

King Willis does not seem to hear him. "Sweet rolls anytime you want," he is murmuring between mouthfuls. "What a lovely life."

What a lovely life indeed.

Prince Virgil turns to leave, the sweet taste of the treat turning sour in his mouth.

The message comes through a knock on the door, each home's door meticulously tapped in the same precisely precise way. *Come tonight. To the fountain. The passageway beneath the land.*

They used to use candles. Back when Prince Wendell

was set to inherit the throne, they lit candles to communicate with a man they hoped would become a good king who would reign forever. It was always the same message. *Come tonight. To the fountain. The passageway beneath the land.*

Prince Wendell would watch from his window, where he could see all the houses of the village, for it was never the same house that carried the message. That, after all, would appear suspicious. It happened at different times as well, if, perhaps, the prince was late getting to his window or was watching early one day. The villagers would watch from their windows, too, for the answer that came in light and darkness and the spaces between.

And then there came a night when the answer never flickered. One home after another sent out its message, but Prince Wendell never made it to his window. He was gone. Banished. Forever lost. The people of the village met in their regular meeting place, but their prince never came.

The next day, they learned that King Sebastien had banished his kind son for the very favor they were asking him the night before. Helping the people. Providing new blankets. Giving them an extra loaf of bread of two.

And so they had stopped using candles, for they had been discovered. The little girl, Clarion, had told of their call. But she had not told of their place.

The villagers are resourceful and imaginative and wise in a way the kingdom did not anticipate. They found another way, thanks to Arthur. Though the night guards know about the candlelight, they do not know about the knocks. The village people have not used the knocks in many years, but she knows, now, that it is time.

They will recognize her knock, of course. And because the village has grown dark in these days after the roundup of its children, no one will see her moving to every door. And because the night will yet grow darker still, no one will see the villagers steal away to the hiding place they have managed to keep secret all these years.

Tonight, the message is delivered in three long taps, a breath, five quick taps, another breath, two taps, breath, five taps, breath, one tap more.

They know what it means, the ones who are listening.

And this, dear reader, is what lifts some of them from their beds. It is what slides past the grief and begins to bloom into something akin to hope.

It is what sends Death away from their doorways for another time or another place or another day.

Miraculous taps.

There are some who do not feel as hopeful as those villagers, however, for they have not heard the taps, and even if they had, they would not know what the stirrings mean.

The children down deep in the bowels of the castle, have grown tired of the darkness. Children are not known to like darkness anyway, but it is always made better when a loving mother or father is near. Though there is a prophet or two or five for every child in this dungeon, though the prophets' arms wrap around the children and keep them warm as their blankets once did, there is not a single mother or father here. And this is what dampens the children's eyes tonight.

They are afraid, dear reader. They are afraid of the infinite blackness. They are afraid that they will never again see light. They are afraid that they will never again see their parents.

They are trapped in a place that could easily be forgotten. They do not know how many days it has been. They do not know one hour from another. Sometimes they wake and there is a bit of bread waiting for them. Sometimes they can hear the footsteps that belong to the one tasked with delivering them their water for the day. Sometimes, when the door far, far above them opens, they have the faintest glimpse of the light they miss almost as much as they miss their parents. Or perhaps it is only their imagination.

The prophetess, truth be told, has never liked the dark, either, but she is fully grown. So it is her voice that cuts through their silent weeping. "It will not be forever, children," she says.

But she knows, of course, that children cannot always sense the passage of time as those with more years can. She knows that it has been eight days since they were locked in a dark dungeon, but she knows that to children, eight days can feel like a whole lifetime.

"But what if it is?" a voice cries out. It is young. Perhaps seven? Younger? Aleen cannot tell. Such a shame that this young child has come to live in a place so dark and damp. If there were light in this dungeon, the children would see Aleen's wild black plaits bouncing as she shakes her head. Such a shame.

"We know it will not be," another voice says. A man. Confident. Gentle. Aleen thinks, perhaps, she has heard this voice before, but without the light, without the face, she cannot know for sure. It has been more than one hundred years, after all, since she was that girl.

"Remember," the man says. "We can See."

"You can see in the dark?" another voice asks. A child, older. Perhaps eleven.

"No, child," the man's voice says. "We can See the future."

"Who are you?" Aleen says. "I believe the children would like to know your name, sir."

The man shifts. She hears him moving toward her. She is sure he has a child draped around him, for every prophet here does.

"I am called Yerin," he says.

"That is a funny name," another child says. Aleen smiles, but of course no one sees.

"Yes. It is," Yerin says.

"Tell us what you See, Yerin," Aleen says. She asks, because she cannot See right now. There is only black for her, and that has made her believe that she will be in this dungeon longer than the others, perhaps. Or that there is something dangerous she must do. Or that she will die. Prophets See black when Death draws near.

There was a time, before she came to this castle, when she could See a whole year into the future, where most prophets See only a few months at most, but her Seeing vanished when they took the book the Old Man gave her. It was a diary of sorts, some three thousand pages. She did not think much of it back when the man who walked her down these stairs had taken it gently from her hands. She would not have been able to read it in this dungeon's dark, after all.

But now, because the pictures have fallen from her mind's eye, she suspects that the book holds some mysterious connection to her power. She lost her power when she lost the book. If she could get it back, somehow.

If she could get it back.

How might she get it back?

Her eyes have grown dark. Aleen has grown off-center. And so it is that she searches in this one called Yerin.

"I See us out in the yard of the castle," Yerin says. "The sun is so bright our eyes cannot stand it. I See us eating hot bread with butter and sweet rolls and great platters of grapes and roast lamb and boiled greens."

The children have grown quiet in the telling. Aleen supposes most of them are asleep. It is better for them to sleep, in a place this dark, though they will wake to nothing better than this.

Yerin's voice grows softer, as if he has noticed, too, the change in the children's breathing, and then the change in the other prophets' breathing. "I See us returning to our homes and hugging the people we love most and reading our storybooks and sleeping in our own blanketed beds," he says.

Aleen does not know how much of this he has really Seen and how much he has said for the sake of the children. But she is overcome by such a longing for her books and her bed that she must close her eyes.

She falls into a long, deep sleep, the kind of sleep that does not take notice of a freezing floor and the absence of a blanket or the shifting sounds bodies make or a light breaking through dark.

Wink

Maude and Arthur met when they were quite young by the standards of our world, but not so very young by the standards of theirs. Arthur was a traveling man by then who had journeyed around the farthest reaches of the seven kingdoms, selling his wood art, making fine furniture and beautifying the worlds of peasants with his craftsmanship. That's how Maude liked to tell it, that is. And then, one day, he showed up on her father's doorstep.

Her father was the village leader in White Wind. The king of White Wind was a kindly man who did not get involved with the village grievances, and so it was Maude's father who presided as judge over arguments as silly as "That child dropped an apple core on my lawn" to those more serious in nature: "My sheep wandered into his pasture and died." The people of White Wind were not so peaceable as those in other kingdoms, so her father had quite a responsibility keeping good relations between neighbors. Maude used to sit in on some of the meetings, held in the town inn, over ale and bratwurst. Mostly the men talked, though the widows were known to put in a few words as well. Maude, for her part, hated the petty conflicts. She did not find it so difficult to get along with a fellow neighbor, if one was not constantly nit-picking about the ways others live their lives. But the people of White Wind did not seem to understand this simple freedom. She wanted nothing more than to escape this wretched kingdom.

She was no fool. She saw her opportunity to escape when Arthur, a young, foreign, vibrant man, knocked on her door.

He was slightly older than she was, twenty to her nineteen. She was past the wedding age for most women of her time. Plenty of the village men had asked, for Maude was considered a lovely woman, with sandy hair and shining caramel eyes, and, also, sufficient and smart. But her father needed her at home. Or so she told herself. She did not exactly know why her father had not wed again after her mother died. Maude did the best she could for him. She cleaned, but it was not a precise cleaning. She cooked, but not so very well as the widow Rayna, who occasionally brought a meal to their door. Maude had seen Rayna's longing as she watched Maude's father go about his business in the town. Why did her father not wed the widow, who was good and kind and young enough to bear him more children?

Maude often wished that her father would marry again so that she could live her life as she very well pleased, traveling the lands instead of trapped in the village of White Wind, where all that happened was a neighbor stealing an apple from another neighbor's apple tree.

And then came the visitor who set it all in motion.

Arthur was handsome, with ruddy brown hair that always looked as if he had just risen from his bed, as if he did not own a comb at all—not tangled, but windswept. It was understandable, of course, for he slept on the ground. Being a man of little means, he had grown accustomed to sleeping beneath the stars, for inns cost money he did not have.

And so it was that one day Maude opened the door to the most piercing blue eyes she had ever seen in all the land, nearly glowing eyes, and there he was. He looked twice, and then he smiled, his whole face carrying the sun in it.

"Your father around, my young lady?" he said, though she knew even then, even with only a glance at his boyish face, that he could not have been much older than she. He leaned against the doorway, crossing his arms across his chest.

"Who might be asking?" she said. She had spirit, that was what the villagers said of Maude. It was what her mother had always said. Spirit that could run wild on a whim or be tamed with a story. The baker's apprentice, Benny, was the first man to appreciate that spirit, but he did not suit her, though her father, at the time, urged her to accept Benny's proposal of marriage. Benny was much too arrogant for her taste. She preferred a man who knew his worth and yet did not tell everyone about it. She preferred a man who recognized the value of women in his life, and Benny was not one of those men. He wanted a wife who was beautiful simply so he could show her off and keep her locked in a house, cooking, cleaning, caring for the children she would bear him. So she had refused to marry him. That had been a spirited argument, shaking the walls of her home, when she told her father of her decision. But he could not ask her to marry for anything other than love, could he? After all, he had loved her mother.

There was something else Maude had not told a single

person, not that she had friends to tell. She had not even written it in her record book, where she penned thoughts from her days, the only real ritual that meant anything at all to her. Every night, she sat by the fireside with a quill pen and the stack of parchment bound by sturdy thread and wrote a page, perhaps two, and then stuffed the book beneath her straw mattress.

The something else was this: Maude wanted to marry a man with magic.

She knew the danger, of course. A man with magic was always a danger, for kings would kill to keep their thrones. She did not want to marry a magic man for the kingdom it might one day bring, as one might expect. She wanted to marry a man of magic because no one had ever taught her how to use her own. No one but her father even knew why she kept her mother's staff, propped in a corner of her room.

"Forget it," he had said after her mother had died. "It is good for nothing."

But she knew it was good for something. It had to be good for something. It was a gift, was it not? She touched the staff every night before bed, part of a story she told herself, about how the power was in the staff, not the magician's hands, and in order not to lose it, she must make contact with the wood every chance she had.

Her mother's staff was ancient. It had been passed on for generations, gnarled and rounded at the top, as if a ball lived on the end of it. A message had been etched into the ball, but she could not read the script. It looked as if it had been touched with loving hands too many times. Perhaps someday, when she unlocked the use of her magic, she would know what those words meant.

The man at her door bowed. "I am called Arthur."

"And from where did you come, Arthur?" She had, of course, heard of this Arthur. He had arrived days ago, and already the people had fallen in love with his woodwork.

"Everywhere," Arthur said. "And nowhere."

"Riddles," Maude said. "I have never liked riddles."

"Well then," Arthur said. "Perhaps you will not like me."

Maude knew this was not true. Already she liked this man, the way he smiled as if it was the most natural thing to do. The way he leaned against a door and crossed his arms across his chest. The way he spoke and the gleam in his eye.

Arthur moved a hand behind his back. When it appeared again, he had a yellow rose. "For friendship," he said, and he winked.

And she knew. This man had magic.

She took him in to see her father, who was not only the town leader but was also the town woodworker. She listened to their conversation, standing on her toes behind the door, learned that Arthur had traveled all over the lands but was looking for somewhere to settle down, somewhere to do his woodworking in peace, with another skilled hand, said to be the best in the land (though it was, in fact, Arthur who was the best woodworker in all the land). Maude knew her father was the sort of man who took to compliments, and so she knew that Arthur would be allowed to stay. A thrill wedged into her heart.

Her father, of course, was pleased and said as much. He could use the help, he said. She heard a slap, which she knew to be her father's hand on Arthur's back, for she had seen him do it to the baker's apprentice on occasion.

She smiled. She would not be so keen on leaving for a while yet. First, she must learn the ways of magic. First, she must learn how to use her gift.

When she saw Arthur out of the house, it was dark. And it was only because she was watching him that she noticed him reach beside the door and draw out the walking stick.

No, not a walking stick at all. A magical staff.

He turned at the edge of the yard. She could hardly distinguish him from the darkness. But she did see him reach up, tip his hat and, she imagined, wink.

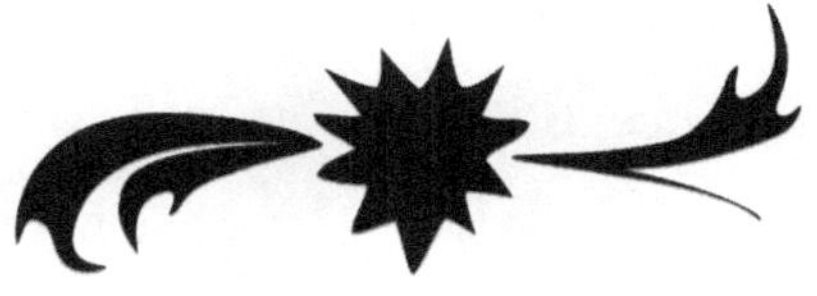

Hope

It might take you all by surprise to know that Arthur and Maude and Hazel and Mercy and twenty-two of the other missing children are, in fact, hiding in the Weeping Woods, closer to home than anyone dared think they would be.

Where are the other seven missing children in our king's register? Well, that is a mystery that will need solving, I am sure you will agree.

Sir Greyson and his entire company of men combed through the woods early on, looking, searching, scouring, really, but they never found the hidden hideout or the haphazard garden or the sheep that had followed Hazel to her new home.

This is as it should be, as Arthur and Maude planned it, as was best to protect the lives of the children. The woods, that day, had closed around them, concealing them from those who were looking. That is the only way they made it. The fairies did not bother them on their way through, though Hazel had watched for them at every turn. A girl of the village had once been carried off to a place called Neverland, a good name for a place where a girl would never see her family and friends again, for she had never been found.

It is a good thing Arthur and Maude did not panic in the mayhem that painted the streets of Fairendale the eve that brought them here. The children were saved, after all, because they had the foresight to make a plan. They called to all the children who had run into the Weeping Woods, momentarily safe from the eyes of the king's guard by the bending of the trees around them. They gathered, sharing their heaving breaths around a circle. They broke, they ran, and then, at precisely the right moment in precisely the right place, the ground opened up.

Arthur had taught the girls well.

Hazel had tried first to create what Arthur asked, but her power was significantly weakened by the disappearance of her twin brother Theo. Twins, you see, cannot practice their magic when separated. So it was Mercy, instead, who had created the house beneath the ground, connected to the earth above it by a tiny shoe, at the behest of Tom Thumb. (We have not yet met Tom Thumb. But his story shall be told soon enough.) Every underground house had a magical portal connecting it to the upper world, where those below could step and suddenly become those above. Tom Thumb took off his shoe, and the children could hardly see where it lay, but Mercy waved her staff anyway, and the dirt swallowed them whole. It was only when they stared at each other, in this hole beneath the ground, that they saw Maude's frontside stuffed with bags of flour and old rags and all the items she could grab that might be turned into food. In the days since their escape, they have lived on bread and water, pulled from the ground beneath them. Mercy, in truth, did not know she had a gift so powerful. But at Arthur's instruction, she had made water flow from the earth. The children had stared at her with gaping mouths.

More than a week has passed. Arthur and Maude and the children have made this underground house a home. The girls have used their magic to make bedrooms, girls on one side and boys on another. They had to make it a comfortable place, for while the king's men searched the forest, they had to remain hidden where no one would expect them to be.

And who would expect them to be living beneath the ground?

When the ground ceased shaking from the presence of soldiers and horses, Arthur moved through the portal, surveying the ground and planning a garden that would not look like a garden at all. They needed more than bread and water, he said. They would need greens, too. A girl named Ruby did the planting.

The sheep had appeared this morning, while Arthur gleaned what vegetables he could for their paltry breakfast. He tried shooing the sheep away, but they refused to leave the woods. Arthur slipped back through the portal miffed. Now he sits before his daughter, thinking aloud.

"They must go," Arthur says.

"They will not," Hazel says. "Not without me."

Arthur looks around at the underground walls, at all the children. His eyes rest on Maude's. They cannot not do a vanishing spell to rid the woods of the sheep, for that will demand far too much strength, but perhaps they can weave another concealment spell for the time being. The children are hungry, though. Another concealment spell will not hold up for long, for magic weakens as its master weakens.

"Ursula," he says.

The girl with raven hair turns to him. "Yes, Mister

Arthur?"

"I need you to do a concealment spell," he says.

"But I have never done a concealment spell," she says, for she knows how advanced a spell such as this one can be.

"No matter," Arthur says. "I will guide you."

"How is it you know so much about magic?" says a boy named Chester. He has a twin named Charles, but they were both born without the gift of magic. Second and third sons. They lost their brother in their race toward the woods. The first brother had always been terrified of the Weeping Woods and the dangers within, though, the day they fled, the Weeping Woods were no match for the king's men. They had seen their brother felled by a sword.

Arthur brushes away the question. There is no time for explaining just yet. Perhaps there will not ever be, for this is not a story he would like to tell.

Ursula crouches next to Arthur. He points to her staff. She raises it up. He holds it, along with her hand. The two of them disappear through the portal.

"No fair," cries another boy, called Jasper. "I want to go out."

They have been beneath the ground for eight days, reader. They have not seen the sun for eight whole days. Can you imagine? They have only sat at tables and reclined in their beds. There has been no running or jumping or laughing, for that matter. The children grow tired and cranky for spending too much time indoors.

"Perhaps one day soon," Maude says. Her words come out in a deep sigh. Hazel locks eyes with Mercy. "For now, we must keep you safe."

Truth be told, this home is better than some of their homes in the village. There is more bread than one could ever want in a day. There is a room for every two children. Some of these children have shared with four or five of their brothers and sisters, so they have more room than ever, though any space with twenty-six people in it would, perhaps, feel cramped, even a space with as many as thirteen rooms.

Still, it is quite astounding, this little home made from a tiny shoe. No man searching the woods will ever find a shoe as small as this one. Tom Thumb is the size of a thumb, as his name suggests. His shoes are the size of a fingernail sliver. Even a seeing glass could not detect a portal so small.

Arthur and Ursula fly through the portal. It is always a surprising return. One never knows where one will drop. Ursula comes in upside down, her staff wrapped around her ankle. She hits the ground with the top of her head. Arthur lands on his rump right beside her.

"Well?" Maude says. "Did you get rid of them?"

"It is a temporary fix," Arthur says. "But, for now, they are concealed."

The children look at Ursula. Mercy, though, turns away. She is jealous of this honor. She would like to have been asked. Arthur did not ask her, you see, because she is the child who made them a home and brought forth water from the ground. Every use of magic weakens its master for a time. She is needed for water and for maintaining the connection with the portal. She must preserve her strength.

But this is not how Mercy sees it. Hazel pats her friend's hand.

"The children would like to go out," Maude says. She looks at Arthur. He looks at her. He shakes his head.

"We must wait for a time," Arthur says. He turns to the children. "I know you are growing restless. But we must wait for a time. We must make sure it is safe. The hour is late, and the woods grow dark." He does not say more.

And the children, because they love and trust this man who saved them from the king's guard, do not say another word. They know of the dangers in these woods that have nothing to do with the men who search for them.

Arthur holds up a thick branch. "I found this out there. I think it will serve us well. Now. Who wants to make me a proper table?"

The girls rush toward him, and, in the end, it is a girl called Minnie who gives him a table. Arthur sets to work on the intricate designs he is known for carving in the village. He bends and carves and brushes wood away until it is time to take from the garden what is theirs for the day.

Day and night and day and night, this is the life of the children living beneath the ground. No one knows they are here. No one knows they are alive.

No one knows that a rider is coming.

Prince Virgil sits alone in his bedchamber. It is large and roomy, about the size of Hazel and Theo's humble cottage.

Hazel and Theo. He misses his friends. Especially Theo. Longing curls around his throat.

If one were to peer inside the door of Prince Virgil's chambers, one would first notice the extravagance. The walls are painted with spectacular flourishes, blue against a color the same shade as the cream Cook warms on the evenings Prince Virgil asks for his sleeping draught. The bed is clothed with the finest blue velvet, which was Prince

Virgil's favorite color as a boy, though he has since favorited green. The bed itself is large enough to accommodate a whole family. It is sunken the slightest bit, right up its middle, where Prince Virgil sleeps, most nights, with his face toward the golden ceiling.

One would also see a boy, sitting in the place where he is most known to lie, his legs crossed beneath him. One would see him turning something over and over in his hands. If one were to draw closer to the boy, one might see that what he holds is a mysterious talisman, carved in the shape of a blackbird, tied onto a blue string. One would see the tears, glistening jagged paths down his smooth cheeks.

Where did he get this talisman, one might wonder?

Nowhere, our prince might reply, for the truth, dear reader, is much more difficult for our prince to embrace. The talisman, you see, was given to him by his best friend, on a birthing day two years ago. Even now, as he sits cross-legged on his bed, turning this talisman over and over and over again in his hands, he is trying to convince himself that the blackbird really did come from nowhere, that a boy called Theo, who happened to be a good friend, never even existed at all. For believing this new reality, though it is not a reality at all, is easier for our prince than the knowledge that his best and only friend might possibly die

—because of him. To create a new reality, where a boy named Theo never existed in the first place, is to absolve himself of all guilt.

And yet, there is this talisman, given for protection. Given for friendship. Given for love.

He remembers well the evening his friend placed it in his hands. "Where did you get this?" he had asked Theo.

"Someone gave it to my father long ago," Theo had said. "For protection in his wanderings."

"That is odd," Prince Virgil said. "A blackbird for protection?"

"Yes," Theo had said. "Blackbirds do not mean in other lands what they mean to Fairendale." To Fairendale, blackbirds mean death.

"I could not wear this," Prince Virgil had said. "It would not bring me protection."

"It is a magical talisman," Theo had said. "It will protect you always."

"But my grandfather," Prince Virgil had said. "He was killed by a blackbird."

Theo, of course, had heard the stories. He did not quite believe them. A man killed by a blackbird? What sort of curse might that have been?

"All the more reason to wear a blackbird around your

neck," Theo had said.

And Prince Virgil could not argue. He had placed the blue string about his neck and felt it grow warm against his chest. "I will have to hide it from my father," he had said. "He does not like blackbirds."

"Yes," Theo had said. "I imagine that is so."

Today, in his room, alone, Prince Virgil stares at the talisman, at the inscription etched in the back of its iron. "For Prince Virgil," it says. "May your days be long and prosperous." And though he tries to forget the words, they are etched, too, in his memory, for what kind of friend would give a prince a talisman for protection, when all he planned to do was steal his throne? It is not the Theo Prince Virgil knows and remembers. And so he must, as they say, kill the Theo he knows and remembers, if only from his memory.

Prince Virgil hurls the talisman across the room. He does not need the sort of protection Theo intended. He will not wear it any longer. The talisman hits the floor with a hollow sound, a sound that feels very much like his heart's beat, knocking around against walls that will not hold it. The talisman slides to a stop beneath a mahogany chest of drawers, one that Theo's father made. Prince Virgil closes his eyes.

Everywhere he looks, there are reminders of the friend he loves. He must do something about that, demand new furniture, sleep in a new room, forget. He must forget.

A knock sounds on the door, two quick raps and a pause. It is the knock of his mother, and for once, he is not glad. She is too good, too kind for him. He will pretend to be asleep. He turns over, staring at a wall he does not see. And it is too bad he does not see it, for this wall holds answers to the wonderings of our prince's mind. If he were to look closely, if he were to really see, as has not happened yet before, he might notice the stories this wall tells. But, for now, its message is lost on him.

Queen Clarion opens the door. "Oh," she says. "I am a bit late tonight. I thought you might be asleep." She crosses the room to his bedside. How did she know he was not sleeping? Well, you see, Queen Clarion opens this door every night, when Prince Virgil is sleeping. Our queen knows that her son sleeps with his face to the sky.

She sits on his bedside. Her hand strokes his cheek. She does not say a word for a time, and then, finally, when his eyes do not close but simply stare without seeing, she says, "You sat in court with your father today?"

Prince Virgil looks at her now. He sees her. He sees her beautiful golden hair and the crown tucked into its silken threads. He sees her blue eyes, the color of the Violet Sea tributary when it catches the evening's glow. He sees the jewels around her neck, flickering in the candlelight.

"Yes," Prince Virgil says. He is still unsure what he thinks about what he saw in court today, but he dares not say it aloud.

"Your father," Queen Clarion says, but she does not say more. Queen Clarion does not like speaking an ill word about another, though she could very well say plenty about her husband. Still, she understands him. She knows from where he comes. And this, you see, makes all the difference.

"He ordered another search," Prince Virgil says. "To find the missing children."

"I fear the children will not be found," Queen Clarion says. "Or, rather, I hope." She says the words softly and looks at her son. He looks at her, knowing that she would understand if he were to say what is in his heart. But to say what is in one's heart takes great courage, and our prince does not feel great courage this eve. So, instead, he looks toward the talisman. It remains hidden from him, clenched in shadows.

What he would say if he had the courage are three very simple things:

He misses his friends.

He does not believe Theo means to steal the throne.

He wishes he could be an ordinary boy.

These are three simple things a prince of Fairendale should not think. He is the heir to the throne. It is an honor to rule a kingdom as lovely as Fairendale. And he found it such, for a very long time, until his father decided that the way to keep rule in a kingdom was to round up the children he had loved for his entire life.

Though, it must be said, our prince, when in the company of his father, longs for the throne more than anything in this world. One might say he is enchanted with power when in the company of the king. One might say he is, perhaps, enchanted with kindness when in the company of his mother. Who is it, dear reader, our prince would rather remain in the company of? Who is it who will win this indecision?

"You have been sitting with your father more often of late," Queen Clarion says, as if she is merely making an observation.

"He would like me to learn the ways of the kingdom," Prince Virgil says.

His mother's eyes fall on him. They do not change, though her voice does, a slight edge to it now. "And what are the ways of the kingdom, my son?"

This is a question our prince is not ready to answer. For, you see, he has not spent enough time learning the ways of the kingdom. It is only of late that he has spent any time at all in the courts, and that is most likely because his friends have disappeared. There is nothing better for him to do anymore. His father is more and more pleased, every day, by his presence.

Queen Clarion seems to understand that her son cannot make his answer yet. She pats his hand. "You will learn in time," she says. "You will decide for yourself. You are nearly a man."

Prince Virgil does not want to be a man yet. He is not fully done being a child. He does not desire the responsibility that comes with ruling a kingdom. He does not think he will ever want that responsibility, if it means imprisoning children and forsaking friends to keep a power that is not his.

"Would you like to hear a story?" Queen Clarion says.

And though Prince Virgil is twelve, an age at which children begin to believe they are too old for stories told aloud by their parents, our prince desires one tonight. It is the missing of his friend. It is the promise of a kingdom, weighing heavily on his shoulders. It is the sadness, moving about in his memory. Stories, of course, have a magical quality about them. They cure sickness, and they calm concern, and they smooth away sadness. One has merely to listen, and words will wander in like soothing balm.

"Yes," Prince Virgil tells his mother. "Yes, I would like a story, please." Our prince has not forgotten his manners. He remembers how to be kind and how to speak politely and how to love when he is with his mother.

Queen Clarion smiles. She pulls the heavy blue velvet up to her boy's chin. These are her favorite moments, when she is granted time alone with her son, when she can wrap him in the warmth of words and mend a heart whole again.

"It is cold in here," she says, glancing toward the window. "It is growing colder."

Prince Virgil looks toward the window as well. "I forgot to close it."

"No matter," Queen Clarion says. She rises swiftly from her place and closes the window before stoking the fire and sitting back on his bedside. "The fire will warm you soon." She smooths the velvet around him again. "What kind of story would you like to hear?" Prince Virgil's candle, balanced on his bedside table, flashes in her eyes. "Perhaps one of adventure? Or love?"

"A happy one," Prince Virgil says. "One that is true."

Queen Clarion does not know many true stories that are happy. But she can modify, perhaps, for there is one that began very happily indeed. So she tells him of his Uncle Wendell, how she was brought to the castle when she was only a girl of six, to marry him. Her mother gave strict instructions that the marriage would wait until she was old enough, sixteen at least, and in those intervening years Prince Wendell taught Queen Clarion to shoot a bow and aim at the place that would be most merciful to the animals hunted, that would take them down in the swiftest way possible so that there would be no pain, or not much of it. Prince Wendell taught her to see what she could not see before.

Queen Clarion hesitates for a moment. She comes to a place in the story where she has always told what she was expected to tell. She has never told the real part of the story before, but something about the way her son looks at her this night tells her now is precisely the right time to tell it. She must share the truth. She must show him the kindness and courage and love of his uncle. She must erase the story of foolishness and tell, instead, the story of a hero, for that is what Prince Wendell was.

So, rather than the typical turn in this story, Queen Clarion weaves another one around her son. She tells of a girl and a boy sneaking from the castle to visit the people of the village, who were starving under King Sebastien's reign. She tells of magic that helped fill their bellies and keep them warm. She tells of the castle and its extravagance, and the scant provisions it would provide to the people who made furniture and shoes and baked bread for the kingdom's pleasure.

It is a story of injustice, where Prince Virgil has only been told a story of might.

"The people could not feed their families with what the castle provided," Queen Clarion says. "They were desperate. Your uncle urged King Sebastien to do something about it. King Sebastien refused."

"Why?" Prince Virgil says. "When the people were starving?"

"Your grandfather believed that the working people should remain the working people," Queen Clarion says.

"But they were working," Prince Virgil says. "And they were still starving."

His mother smiles, but it is a sad smile. "Precisely," Queen Clarion says. "Your uncle could not watch his people starve. His heart was too tender." Her eyes take on a faraway look. "Your grandfather believed that meant your Uncle Wendell was weak."

"So Grandfather sent him away?" Prince Virgil says. "For having a tender heart?"

"For helping the people," Queen Clarion says. "Your uncle helped them survive."

"I do not understand," Prince Virgil says.

"It is not for us to understand," Queen Clarion says, for this is something she has learned in all the years since, in all the years grieving for a man she had grown to love, though she had only recently turned seven when Prince Wendell left, in all the years married to his brother, who had been trained to be another King Sebastien, only larger and, perhaps, just a touch softer. "It is for us to do better." Notice, dear reader, that she does not tell him what the better thing to do is. She leaves that open to him, for deciding what to do can only happen in one's own mind.

"Was my grandfather afraid of the villagers?" Prince Virgil says.

"Perhaps," Queen Clarion says. "Perhaps he feared the same thing your father fears."

"Losing the throne?" Prince Virgil says.

Queen Clarion bends her head. She takes her son's hand. "There are more important things to life than keeping a throne."

They are words, you may remember, from another time

and another place. Queen Clarion is a wise woman. She knows much of the world, much more than, say, her son. Her words dip into his chest, squeezing softly. He knows them to be true. He blinks tears away. There is a great, wide chasm on his insides. He fills it with more words.

"I loved Theo," Prince Virgil says. "He was my best friend."

"Losing a friend is not easy," Queen Clarion says.

"Do you think he is alive?" Prince Virgil says.

His mother touches his cheek. "We cannot say for sure," she says. "But if the boy had magic, we can hope."

"If he had magic, he could take what is mine," Prince Virgil says.

"Perhaps," Queen Clarion says. "What do you think?"

Prince Virgil thinks about this boy he knew, this boy he loved. He thinks about the sister with evening sky eyes, and the way she could turn a cloudy day into one that held the brightest sun a world has ever seen. He thinks about the girl with flaming red hair. "No," he says. "No, I do not think he would have. But he did lie about his magic."

"Fear makes man do unexplainable things," Queen Clarion says. "Look what his magic set in motion."

Prince Virgil considers this. Children stolen from their homes. Families torn apart. Parents beaten in the streets.

So much destruction from a simple discovered secret.

"What happened to the people?" Prince Virgil says. His mother tilts her head, as if she does not understand. So he says, "After my uncle left?"

"They carried on," she says. "As people do."

"But if he cared so much about the people, why did he leave them?" Prince Virgil says. "Why did he not stay and help them?"

Queen Clarion smiles again. "I suppose your uncle had other plans," she says. "And the people have done well enough for themselves."

Prince Virgil supposes that, yes, they had. They did not have quite enough to eat, but they had found ways around it. A community garden he had only seen once. Some sheep for wool. Goats for milk. A wheat field behind the village.

"Does he still live?" Prince Virgil says.

"We have not seen your uncle since he was banished," Queen Clarion says. "But I suspect he lives still."

"You miss him," Prince Virgil says.

His mother's eyes turn soft. "Yes," she says. "I loved your uncle very much. He was kind to me."

Prince Virgil wonders, at this moment, why he has never heard this story before. He asks.

"There is a story your grandfather wanted told," Queen Clarion says. "It is the same story your father wanted told." She pauses for a moment. "You were not ready to hear the truth. But I thought, perhaps, that now you are."

And this is precisely what urges him to ask the question that has weighed on his mind since turning that talisman over and over and over again in his hands.

"Did Grandfather really die from a blackbird?" Prince Virgil says.

"Is that the story your father has told you?" Queen Clarion says.

"It is the story the villagers tell," Prince Virgil says. "Father does not tell stories. He leaves that to others."

"Yes, I suppose he does," Queen Clarion says. She takes a breath, lets it out smoothly. She smells of peppermint. She leans down to kiss him goodnight, for this is a story that will wait for another evening. "Your grandfather died of the heart sickness," she says.

She is all the way across the room when Prince Virgil calls out, "Will I die of the heart sickness?" Queen Clarion stops in the doorway. Her gown swishes as she turns. She looks at her son. He looks at her.

"I do not believe you will," she says. "I believe you will

live for a very long time." His mother closes the door, leaving her words with him.

And these words, dear reader, ease our prince from his bed and around to the chest of drawers and down to the floor. He slides his hand between the gap of wood and floor, and when he grasps the talisman, he carries it back to his bed, where he falls asleep with his fingers wound tight around it.

While the boy is sleeping, his father, the king, remains in the court, still eating, supping this time, for the fifth time, with his captain of the guard, who has not had a decent meal in months.

Sir Greyson, good man that he is, tries not to eat too much or too swift, tries to think of his soldiers, still camping on the castle grounds, roasting fish from the stream beside the castle on fires spread around the palace lawn. They have not been permitted to go home as yet, have not even seen their families until further orders can be given. The king has forbidden their respite. And so it is that Sir Greyson tries to think of his men.

But it has been so long since he has had roast lamb in a rich buttercream sauce like this one that he cannot help reaching for more once his portion has fully and rapidly disappeared. He does not, in fact, have to reach at all. He simply puts his fork down for one moment, and Garth, who is a quite excellent page, fills his plate again. So, you see, it is not entirely his fault that he eats until he is nearly bursting.

"Good man," the king says, nodding toward Sir Greyson's plate, filled for the third time.

"Please," Sir Greyson says. He waves Garth away. "No more." He will surely burst were he to eat any more.

The king has asked his captain of the guard to supper for the sole purpose of informing him of the decree he intends to send to neighboring kingdoms, ordering them to surrender any fugitives who have come into their lands in the weeks past. He does not seek approval, mind you. He merely seeks a face colored in embarrassment, perhaps, for not having thought up this grand idea in spite of wearing the name Captain of the King's Guard, tasked with finding all the missing children (though Sir Greyson and his men have already visited the neighboring kingdoms and, as you might recall, came away with no children). King Willis merely seeks praise, for an idea so carefully and perfectly wrought (though he was not the first to consider it). He merely wishes to show his captain how dire this situation has become (though nothing has changed, dear reader).

"Captain," the king says. He is a man given to warming up a conversation. "Tell me your plans."

Sir Greyson clears his throat. He considers the meeting before supper, all the words already spoken. Does he have more to say? Perhaps?

"We will begin closer to home," Sir Greyson says.

"Begin again," King Willis says. He stares at his man from across the table, his lips pulled up into a smile that resembles a sneer. Do you know what a sneer is, dear reader? It is a most horrid thing, particularly on the face of a king. Particularly on the face of a king such as this one. Particularly when the only light in a room is the candle flickering on the table.

Sir Greyson shivers, tensing his legs as if to run at any moment. And it is true that King Willis looks dangerous, more like an animal than a man in this dim light, with that horrid sneer. The two men are seated at a long table, Sir Greyson near the end, though not all the way, for the ends of tables like these are intended for those in powerful positions. Sir Greyson is not powerful, compared to King Willis. Prince Virgil, on the nights he sups with his father, has taken to sitting at the empty end, directly across from the king, though one might argue that "directly across" is not the same measurement as "ten feet across." Sir Greyson sits at the prince's imaginary elbow, for the prince is not supping so late but is, as we have seen, tucked in his bed, with a wooden talisman clutched in his hand.

"Yes, I suppose it would be beginning again," Sir Greyson says.

"What is that you say, my good man?" King Willis calls from the other end of the table.

Sir Greyson looks at his king. "Yes," he says, louder this time. "We shall begin again."

"And I," the king says. He makes a grand gesture with his arms. The skin pulses against the sleeves of his royal robes. Sir Greyson is momentarily distracted, thinking about the king he first came to know. He was nothing like this large king, this king who has grown overly large and soft and insatiable. How did it happen? When did it happen? Why did it happen? King Willis reaches for yet another piece of bread.

The once smaller king, though never, perhaps, small at all (and it must be said, dear reader: Largeness is a perfectly wonderful thing, so long as the largeness is not the result of greed and power and selfishness, as it seems to be for King Willis), has been replaced by a king who will soon not fit through the doorways, should his growth continue.

"What do you think of that?" King Willis says. Sir Greyson takes a sharp breath. Has his king been talking all this time?

"I am sorry sir," Sir Greyson says, deciding to be an honest man about it. "I believe the food has shored up my ears. I did not hear you in your entirety."

The king stares at him, his mouth open in what must be shock, but then he shakes out a long, bellowing laugh. "Shoring up your ears," he says, when his laugh has turned to silence. "I did not know my captain of the guard was so funny." He looks at Sir Greyson, his eyes squinting, his mouth in a line now. "Take care. Your king is speaking."

Sir Greyson listens to King Willis ramble on and on about a decree and how it will get to the neighboring kingdoms and what he will do to the kingdoms should he discover they are hiding the children of Fairendale within their borders. And when he is finished, he looks expectantly at his captain of the guard.

"Well, sir? What say you?" the king bellows across the table.

Sir Greyson clears his throat. "I do not advise taking action just yet," Sir Greyson says. "With all due respect, sire."

"And why not?" King Willis says. "Perhaps they need to

hear from a powerful king, rather than his servant men."

A sliver of anger climbs up Sir Greyson's throat.

Firstly, Sir Greyson does not consider King Willis a powerful king, for a powerful king, in Sir Greyson's mind, is a wise one. Secondly, he does not appreciate being called a servant. He is a paid man, of course, but he does not do menial tasks. He does noble tasks. He protects the kingdom. He risks his life. He searches for children.

A sharp pain splits his throat. No. That is not so noble, now, is it?

Still, a servant? He is no servant. But, fortunately, Sir Greyson is an intelligent man and knows better than to argue with his king. At least about something as small as being called a servant.

For something as large as a decree that could very well bring war upon the land, it is another story entirely.

"I must disagree with you, my lord," Sir Greyson says. "We have traveled to the lands already. I do not think they would appreciate hearing from our king so soon." Particularly when "hearing from our king" means interpreting veiled threats. Sir Greyson does not say this aloud, however.

"What would you have me do, then?" King Willis says. "I have been counseled otherwise."

"By whom?" Sir Greyson says, for he did not know that King Willis had counselors at all.

King Willis waves his hand. "That makes no matter," he says.

The king and Sir Greyson stare at one another for a time. There is no sound at all in the royal dining hall. Even the servants hold their breaths.

"Sire," Sir Greyson says. "I must beg you to reconsider."

"What is it I must reconsider?" King Willis says.

"Our relationship with the other kingdoms," Sir Greyson says.

"We are the fairest kingdom of them all," King Willis says. "The most powerful."

And while it is true that Fairendale may once have been the most powerful kingdom, part of the land's power was found in its children, in its magic flashing about the streets. Its children are gone. It has not much power left. Though there is some power left yet.

Oh, yes.

"Pardon me, your highness," Sir Greyson says. "I implore you to wait. At least until my men and I have a chance to comb the Weeping Woods again. Until we have searched the village. Until we enlist the mermaids down by the cove, in case any children might have ventured into the Violet Sea."

King Willis gives a great laugh once more. "Children in the Violet Sea," he says. "That is quite preposterous."

Sir Greyson can see that his king is unsure now. "I am certain they are closer to home," Sir Greyson says. "I am certain that is why my men did not find them. Please permit us to try once more before sending this decree."

King Willis nods. "Very well," he says. "You have one week. If you do not find the children in one week, the decree will fly."

Sir Greyson will make haste. He does not want war to hit the land. He had heard stories about war. He knows what it can do to men and women. He knows what it can do to children. What it had done to him, though that was not a war against men but one against the elements of a dangerous land.

"We will begin in the forest, at first light," Sir Greyson says.

"Tonight," King Willis says.

Sir Greyson does not think he can ask his men to do such a thing, not only for the dangers held within the Weeping Woods but also for the exhaustion his men, at this very moment, feel in their very bones, for Sir Greyson feels it in his own. But he can see the king's patience is growing short. "Yes, sire," he says. "As you command."

"Search under every stone," King Willis says. "Examine every creature, even the tiny ants. The children have magic on their side. They could be pesky squirrels by now, for all we know. Or raccoons or porcupines." King Willis reaches for another slice of bread. He takes a large bite before he says, with a muffled sound, "Find them."

Sir Greyson rises from his seat, trying to erase the sight of bread crumbs spraying from his king's mouth. He would round up every creature he could find. His men would set traps. They would hide out in the forest, even after the sun's setting. But they would begin tomorrow, at first light.

His king would never know.

When Sir Greyson reaches the door, he suddenly remembers the bellies of his men. He turns around. The king has finished his bread in record time. Steaming plates of lamb and bread and smoked potatoes cover the long table. The king has more than enough food. Sir Greyson will ask to take some to his men.

"Sire," Sir Greyson says. The king looks up.

"Yes?" he says. "Why are you still here, Captain?"

"My men," Sir Greyson says. "They are hungry, sire. Might I take them some food?"

King Willis looks at his captain. Sir Greyson feels his king's gaze slicing through him, dividing him clean in half so he is not so much a man as he is a trembling child. He would turn and go, but his king holds him in a look that feels unbreakable.

"You," King Willis says, his voice very like what men have said of the Violet Sea: cold, dark, unmerciful. "Dare to ask me if I will share my food with the common man?"

"I am sorry, You Highness," Sir Greyson says, and the words come tumbling out, end over end, on their own. "My men are hungry. And we have all traveled so—"

"You dare ask me if I will share my food with the common man?" King Willis roars. It is a chilling roar. The marble floors of the castle nearly shake in its great, wide breath.

"Please, sire," Sir Greyson says. "Let it be as if I had never asked."

The king is still bellowing when Sir Greyson turns and flees out the door. He should have stuffed his pockets with bread. At least then he would have something to share. Now he will bid his men good night with a full belly, while they sleep starving.

Perhaps they will find something in the woods on the morrow.

Sir Greyson returns to the castle grounds, where his men have disappeared into their tents for the night. He looks toward the village, where his mother is probably sleeping now. He misses his mother. He has not seen her in so long. Does she live? Surely someone would have gotten word to him if she does not. He hopes that someone else has taken to caring for her in his absence. But who? The people have all but died since the children disappeared.

He is turning away when he notices a light glowing in one of the village windows. Strange. It is late for the villagers to be up. He knows their habit of retiring early, preserving their candles and setting their sleep to the sun. He used to be one of them, after all. But, then, the village has changed since the children left it. It has grown quiet. Sad. A bit mysterious, perhaps.

Sir Greyson looks up at the sky and toward his men and back to the village. He tries not to think about what a light in a village window might possibly mean.

A group of villagers gathers on the other side of the hill where they fetch water from a fountain. There is a hidden passage. There are secrets. There are whispers.

Some of them are parents whose children sleep in the dungeons with one hundred forty-three prophets. Some of them are parents whose children went missing, and they have no knowledge of where they are. Some of them are no longer parents but old grandparents with white hair and papery skin. Some of them were never parents in the first place.

What they all wish to know is what will be done to save the children. For someone must save the children. Fairendale, after all, is not the same without children. It is not warm. It is not dry. It is not light.

And perhaps it is not so important who they are or to whom they belong. What is important is that they all, on this particular night, when a rapping on the door stirred them from their fitful sleep, have risen from their beds and walked up the hill and slipped through the secret door and now stand in a candlelit room, hugging the shadowy corners, for they do not want to know who is here and who is not. What is more important than even this is that they are thinking, talking, planning how they might yet save the children, before it is too late.

And it is, perhaps, with great delight that the villagers might look inside the walls of the Fairendale castle, deep, deep down in its bowels, for were they to have a way of seeing what happens behind solid stone doors, they might, perhaps, see a boy named Calvin.

Calvin is Cook's assistant. He is not good for much in the kitchen but cutting vegetables and getting in the way. But the perk of being Cook's assistant is that he sees the crates of food that settle on counters, to be eaten by the royal family. He knows that these crates hold more than enough food for one family of only three people. So he takes a little every day, feeding his own belly.

And then, when he is tasked with keeping the children in the dungeons beneath the dungeons fed and watered, he began to execute a plan on which he had spent quite some time—taking a little, hiding it away, waiting. His storehouse grows daily. So tonight, when Cook dismisses him with a bit of bread that is not nearly enough for all the ones who share a dungeon, Calvin retreats to his store, which is not quite as large as he would prefer, but is, perhaps, enough. He stuffs apples and bits of bread and carrots and whatever he can fit in the pockets of his breeches, beneath his tunic, inside, even, the floppy hat he wears on his head. He balances the expected tray of food and water and does not consider how he might appear to one walking through the castle this night. Fortunately, there is no one walking through the castle tonight, and so he lights a candle, and he descends the stairs, and he can hear their voices of wonder.

"Is that light I see?" a man's voice calls.

"Who is there?" says a woman.

He turns the corner. It is he, Calvin. He has brought food and candlelight and enough water for all of them.

"You," says a woman with what looks like snakes for hair. "You brave boy."

"For you," he says. He empties his pockets and his hat and the tunic, placing before them more food than they have seen in all the days and nights spent in this dungeon. The children murmur, but they do not reach for the food.

An old man stares at him, his hair white and wild. "Why, my boy?" he says. "Why did you risk your life like this? To bring us light?"

"No one can live without light," Calvin says. He has heard this somewhere, back when he was a boy, perhaps, though he does not remember much from that time. He remembers his parents leaving, dying, Cook says, and then he was brought to the castle rather than shipped away to some distant cousin in the kingdom of Ashvale. And lucky for him, for the kingdom of Ashvale was leveled by a red, spitting mountain that soaked the ground with its erupting fire and then cooled into rock. The people burned in their homes when it rained from the sky. And he is here, alive, helping the children.

"What is your name, boy?" the woman says. Her white teeth glow against her dark face, but it is not a frightening glow so much as it is a comforting one.

"Calvin," he says.

"I am called Aleen," the woman says. She moves closer to the prison bars. "Do you know what you have done for us, my boy?"

He has fed them. He has brought them light. Is there more?

"You have brought us light," she says. "You have given us hope."

"I will bring more," Calvin says. "Every night I can." Every night he could steal away from Cook, every time he could stuff his pockets with extra food. Perhaps he could come up with something larger to carry all his supplies, something a person would not notice. Perhaps a knapsack. He would search the old rooms of the castle, where no one had lived for some time. There might be something. He could sew a stitch or two. Cook had seen to that, when his legs began growing too fast and she had no more time to let out his hems.

"You must be careful," Aleen says. "Do not risk your life, boy. You are needed."

Had he not already risked his life? Or very near it. Cook would flay him were she to discover what he had done. He would certainly have to be careful. But what did she mean that he was needed? He had never really been needed in his entire life. Cook made it a habit to remind him of this, that she had never asked for help in her kitchen, that he only made her job harder, that she wished the castle would find another job for him to do.

A child moves to the bars. Her hands wrap around them. She tries to smile, but Calvin can tell she is weak. Her hair hangs in a heavy curtain across her eyes. She brushes it away, but it is as if the strands are permanently stuck there. This is, you see, what weeping in your sleep can do. "Thank you," she says. Her eyes, the parts of them visible beneath her blanket of hair, shine in the candlelight.

Calvin dips his head and shoves the tray forward.

"Might you hand it to us between the bars, my boy?" Aleen says.

Certainly. He had not thought of that. He dumps the food from the saucer onto the tray, hands Aleen the saucer and then begins to give her each piece of food.

"And the light?" says the white-haired man. His black eyebrows furrow around his eyes, as if he is lost in constant thought. Yerin is a thoughtful man, and he has much more time for thinking now than ever, trapped in this dungeon.

Calvin passes the candle between the bars. The man looks at Aleen. "We will have to preserve the light," he says.

"I can get you more," Calvin says.

Aleen nods. "Please do, my boy," she says. She gestures to the children behind her. "The children are afraid of the dark."

He certainly understands that. Calvin, for one, is glad he is not tasked with turning down all the torches of the castle. It is a job for another. He hopes it will never pass to him.

Calvin watches them for a moment. And then he turns to go. He stops at the bottom of the stairs, gazing up at the blind way before him. He did not think about bringing a candle for the return trip up. He looks back at the children, gathered around the tiny bit of light and the extra food laid out before them as if it is a feast. It is, perhaps, a feast for bellies that have not tasted much besides bread and water for so many days.

Surely he can brave the dark this one time? Surely he can make it up one set of stairs, though they number in the hundreds, when the children have sat in darkness for many days? Surely he can summon his courage?

Calvin climbs the stairs, one at a time, careful not to stumble. Creatures scuttle across his path, but he hums a tune Cook is always singing and tries not to think about what they might be or whether they have claws or what might lie in wait for him around the next turn.

He reaches the top and breathes, in, out, in, out, for several moments. It is as if he has won a battle for his life, which, of course, is exactly what battling a fear feels like, is it not?

The castle is dark, but the moon is bright tonight. He finds his way to his rooms easily, stokes the fire and crawls into his bed.

Proposition

Talk reached Maude all over the town, about the man who had showed up in White Wind. He was said to have wrestled bears in the enchanted forests that wound throughout the land. He was said to have battled dragons single-handedly and survived. He was said to have swum the Violet Sea, the very place where so many of the men of White Wind had disappeared on a voyage that had become legendary in their history. Maude did not know how much of it was true. He seemed a bit small for all that.

Arthur made his home at the local inn, which charged a mere penny for every night of stay. Her father, she knew, paid him ten pennies a week, which left him ample money to feed himself, but still Maude brought him bread and porridge and, on occasion, a roast leg of lamb, when her father permitted it at their own table.

Every morning Arthur showed up at her door with a handful of yellow roses and the wink of an eye, and then her father would walk him out to the workshop behind their cottage. Arthur would work all day. Sometimes she would watch him. Sometimes she caught him watching her. She was a beautiful young lady, after all. Perhaps he wondered why she was not yet married, as most of the young ladies her age were. His wondering, however, did not stop his pursuit for her heart.

It did not take much to convince Maude to lose her heart. For many days, as she watched young Arthur whittle his furniture, she could see the magic dripping from his fingers, smoothing an edge here, extending a curl there, widening a leg in the most efficient manner. He had only to touch the wood. She wondered, at first, how this worked, for she had always supposed that magic came from the magician's staff. But when she ventured closer, she noticed the staff propped on his right foot while he worked.

So he had magic enough to use it when the staff did not touch the object he was transforming. It must be powerful magic indeed.

When her father entered the workshop, which was not so often anymore, for he had no need to dirty his own hands with the work (Arthur was not only a skilled craftsman but a quicker woodworker than any had ever seen), Arthur shoved the staff into the shadows. Maude did not think it mattered so much, for her father was not an observant man, and had he noticed the staff, he would have likely thought it was nothing more than a walking stick. That is what it appeared to be, after all. There were no ornate markings. It looked as if, on his travels, Arthur had plucked a branch from a tree and commandeered it into his service. It was curved in the slightest, with a large knobby bump near the top. Old men used sticks such as these to hold their backs straight. Though he was a young man, it was an inconspicuous prop.

Maude watched Arthur and waited for her opportunity.

And one day it came.

Her father had traveled up the village road to visit the king, who had heard of the new woodworker's elaborate furniture and asked about a new bedpost for his son. Her father was negotiating the sale. Arthur worked alone. The king would keep her father for a time, she knew, for theirs was a kind king who served his guests dinner and wine and desserts she had not the capacity to even imagine.

She stood silently in the doorway of her father's workshop for a time, watching Arthur, for she did not want to startle him. What did magic do when it was startled?

Arthur turned a table over and worked on a leg. He put it right-side up and bent eye-level with it to make sure it did not lean. When he faced the doorway, as if sensing someone was there, Maude spoke.

"I want you to teach me," she said.

Arthur smiled, that lopsided grin that turned his eyes smaller. "You want to make furniture?"

She shook her head. "Not furniture. Magic."

He stared at her for a time. He could not possibly think she did not know about his secret. He had, after all, turned the air into a rose at their first meeting. She supposed it could not have been air. There was no magic powerful enough to turn air into something you could touch. She held up her staff. "I have magic, too," she said.

"No one must know I have magic," Arthur said, turning back to his table.

"No one would know," Maude said.

"Hush," Arthur said. "It would be far too dangerous."

"A man like you? Frightened of danger?" Maude said. She did not know quite what to think. A man who had, by the villagers' account, braved bears and dragons and the Violet Sea, afraid of magic?

"You do not know what kings will do to eliminate a magic man from the pages of history," he said.

Yes. Perhaps this was something she did not know. But she knew a place they could go. "I know a place," she said. He looked at her. "No one would know."

"Where is this place?" he said.

"I will show you," she said. "This eve."

He dipped his head. "As you wish," he said.

"And you will teach me?" she said, for he had not yet agreed. Arthur shook his head.

"First, I must see this place for myself," he said. "And then we will make our plan." She knew him, then, to be a man of caution. She admired that about him, but her longing to practice magic did not diminish in light of danger. She would find a way. She must.

"Meet me behind the inn after my father is done with you," she said, and she turned to leave. His voice stopped her in the doorway.

"Tell me," he said. "Why is it that you have never learned magic yourself?"

Maude's skirts shifted as she faced him again. "My mother died when I was a babe," she said. "And my father…" She glanced behind her, as if her father had magically appeared. She lowered her voice. "My father forbade the practice of magic in his house."

"Why?" Arthur said.

Maude shook her head. "I do not know."

"Very well then," Arthur said. "This eve."

Maude returned to the cottage and tried her best to wait patiently for the sun to set, though we know that when one is waiting for something for which one longs, it is not always particularly easy to exercise patience. But Maude set to work on supper, knowing she would likely eat alone, for when her father returned from his castle trips, the wine in his belly always sent him into a deep sleep that would be her gift this night.

Hidden

Sir Greyson and his men move at first light. They comb through the forest, which is not so sinister in the light of day, though it has grown colder in recent days, and the sun does not shine as it did before, when Fairendale still wore vibrant colors rather than muted ones.

And though they feel eyes watching them (the eyes of sprites? Fairies said to lure men to a place where children rule the land? Goblins? Dragons?), they do their work, as the king commanded. Sir Greyson joins them, unwilling to let his men risk their lives, if that is what they are doing, without him.

He knows, this captain, that he and his men cannot hope to possibly catch all of the animals of the forest, though it is, perhaps, what the king expects. And if they were able to catch all the animals in the forest, how would they know which ones were children under a spell of magic?

Sir Greyson strides through the forest. He looks for unusual signs—tracks, a lost scrap of clothing, perhaps, or, better yet, children who have grown tired of hiding. He could never have lasted this long in hiding when he was a child. He admires the children, though they have made his job more difficult. Though they are the reason he has not seen his mother and does not even know whether she lives. Sir Greyson is not a man to hold grudges. And if he were, what justification would there be in holding a grudge against innocent children who merely want to save their own lives? Sir Greyson understands, you see. He knows why they hide. He urges them to hide, in fact, though he would not speak such words aloud to his men or to the king. He does not, in truth, want the children found, for there is a feeling in the pit of his stomach that says it would be nothing but disaster.

Stay hidden, he whispers into the air. *Stay hidden, whatever you do.*

The children, of course, cannot hear our captain, for

they hide, still, beneath the ground, cut off from the forest, protected by a tiny shoe. They can feel the vibrations of horses, the walking of men, the springing of traps, though they do not know them for what they are.

Maude looks at Arthur. "Movement," Arthur says. "Someone is out there."

The children are growing hungry. They have not yet had their breakfast, but they need wood from the forest. Arthur cannot make his daily gathering voyage until the movement ceases. So they wait. And wait. And wait.

Finally, finally, finally the ground grows silent. And still they wait.

"Father?" Hazel says. She looks at Arthur, her blue eyes growing large. "Why must we continue waiting?"

Arthur stares at the ceiling. "To make sure," he says. He looks at Maude. Maude nods her head. "Alright, children. I will gather our supplies for the day."

"Let me go with you," Mercy says. She pushes through the crowd to stand before Arthur.

"Do not be foolish, child," Arthur says. "I am not a child. I am not important to the kingdom."

Maude lets out a sound much like a sob, and the children turn their heads to her, but Arthur pulls her into his arms and hides her face from their eyes. He whispers in her ear. He turns back to the children. "I will return shortly," he says. "Stay here." He pulls away from Maude. She has, it seems, composed herself. He holds her elbows and shakes her gently. "If I do not return," he says. He looks at the children and then back at Maude. "Remain here. Remain hidden."

Maude gives one nod of her head, and then Arthur steps through the portal and is gone.

The children wait. It seems that all they ever do anymore is wait.

And when the waiting grows too long, Mercy jumps from the fold, shouts, "I shall go after him," and disappears through the portal, her staff gripped tightly in her hand.

Maude stares at the place where the girl had been.

Clearing

The sun did finally set, as all suns are wont to do, and Maude slipped out of her father's home when she heard his snores carried on the wind that moved through their windows. Arthur was waiting for her behind the inn.

"We must use no light," Arthur said. "Do you know the way without it?"

"Yes," Maude said. She had traveled this way nearly every day since her mother had died. It was a place, by the river, where her father used to bring her when she was a child, a place he said her mother sat and penned great long letters to her family in Lincastle. No one from the village ventured to this place beside the river, for it was deep in the forest, and many stories had been told of the creatures of the forest. Maude was not frightened. She had been inside many times and had always made it back out.

"Hurry, then," Arthur said, and they both took off running. They reached the woods only by the light of the moon. "In there?" Arthur said.

Maude took his hand. "I know the way," she said. "I have been here many times before." She brought him to the very banks where her mother sat. Arthur looked at the water.

"Part of the Violet Sea?" he said.

"Yes," she said.

"Are there no mermaids in this one?" he said.

"I have never seen them," she said. She had only heard of the magical creatures who lured men to their deaths beneath the waters.

"And you have been here many times," he said. His eyes were difficult to see in the darkness. Though they stood in a clearing, the moon remained hidden behind the trees.

"Yes," she said. They stood for a time, Arthur looking behind them.

"We must be sure no one has followed us," he said.

Maude nodded and waited, while he circled the trees. When he turned back to her, she said. "Is it true that you swam the Violet Sea and lived?"

Arthur laughed. "You cannot believe everything you

hear." But he did not answer one way or another. (In truth, dear reader, no man has ever survived the swimming of the Violet Sea, for there are sea creatures a human eye could never even imagine. But that is a story for another day.)

"No, I suppose you cannot," she said.

"Now," Arthur said. "Magic."

"How is it that you have managed to keep your magic hidden for so long?" Maude said.

"It was not always so," Arthur said. "I did not always need to hide my gift. Until it became a danger."

"Is it not always a danger?" Maude said.

Arthur looked at her. There was something mysterious about his eyes, but perhaps it was simply the moon. "Yes," he said. "I suppose it is." He drew a stick from his pocket, and at his touch, it became a staff. She stared in wonder, having not noticed that he did not carry his walking stick to the woods this night. He had carried it in his pocket instead.

"How?" she said.

"Not everyone can," he said. "I have learned from many masters."

She envied him and his travels. Were she permitted to travel, she might have learned from masters, too.

"I know nothing," she said. "I know only that I possess

the gift."

"I shall teach you," he said. "But it must be our secret."

She could keep a secret. She had been keeping a secret for thirteen years.

Sleep

Arthur is anything but happy to see Mercy. He grabs the girl, throws her behind him.

"Do you see what they have done, child?" he says. "Do you see?"

Mercy looks around. She does not see anything out of the ordinary. There is the forest floor. There is the tiny shoe one could not see if it were not known to be there. There is the spot Ursula spread her concealment spell in the dark of night. But wait. The sheep. She can see the sheep. What had happened to the spell?

She turns to Arthur. "How——" she says.

He points to the tops of the trees. "There," he says. "Up there."

And she sees the rest of the sheep, dangling from nets, bleating from the trees. "How did they come to fly?" she says.

"Traps," Arthur says. "And I am certain there are men watching. We must make haste."

"But what must we do?" Mercy says.

"Cut them down," Arthur says. He slides a dagger from his belt and begins climbing a tree.

"But it is too high," Mercy says. "You will injure them."

"They are no good to us up here," Arthur says. He looks down at her. "And you have magic."

Yes. She does have magic. She will make a soft place for them to land. And this is precisely what she does, following Arthur to every tree, pointing her staff, hiding behind the trunks as he bids her, though she does not know from what she is hiding. If it were men, would they not have seen her by now?

"Take care," Arthur says when Mercy steps behind another tree. "There is one still waiting for its prey."

Mercy glances at the ground. A net, covered in leaves, lies just beside her foot. She steps away. "And how do we hide the cut traps?" Mercy says.

Arthur lets go of the tree he is climbing and thumps to the ground. "We take them with us," he says. "We use them."

"Why are the men not watching their traps?" Mercy

says.

Arthur looks around the forest, as if he, too, has wondered the very same thing. "I do not know," he says. "Perhaps we have fortune on our side. But I do not think it will be for long. Sheep do not roam woods without a shepherd."

"I can cast another concealment spell," Mercy says.

"I fear your strength will be needed for something far more important," Arthur says. "Let the sheep be found." He slaps one on the back, but it does not move. "Go on, then," he says to the animal. "Run."

Though they are in a grave circumstance, Mercy cannot help but smile. "Perhaps they wait for your daughter."

Arthur looks at the girl. "Yes, well," he says. "Hazel will not be coming up."

The air shimmers around them, and suddenly, unexpectedly, the very girl they speak of is before them. She looks from one to the other.

"You are safe then?" she says.

"You children do not listen," Arthur says. "You must listen if you want to keep your lives."

"But you did not come back," Hazel says. "And Mercy did not come back." She looks at her friend. "You should not have come here."

"You should not have come here, either," Mercy says. She holds her head straight and high.

"Both of you," Arthur says. "Back this very moment. I shall be right behind you."

"What about the sheep?" Mercy says. "The shepherdess is here now."

Arthur looks at his daughter. "Yes," he says. "I suppose she is." He takes both of Hazel's hands in his. "I need you to send your sheep away."

"Send them away?" Hazel says. "But we need them."

"There are traps," Arthur says. He holds up one of the nets so she can see. "People have been here. They have been setting traps. They are still looking."

Hazel looks from her father's face to the traps and then to her sheep. "How will we manage?"

"If they stay," Arthur says. "It is only a matter of time before we are found."

"But the portal is tiny," Hazel says. "They will never discover something so small."

"It is far better to take precautions," Arthur says. "Please, daughter. Send them away. I want you all to live. I want you all to pass your days in safety."

"And we will stay in this underground home?" Hazel

says. "We will live here forever? The king will stop looking?"

Arthur shakes his head. "We must get back," he says. "We must make haste." His voice, dear reader, is splintered, pleading, full of sorrows he cannot speak today. "Please."

And because he is her father, because she loves him, because she loves the children who hide behind a tiny portal, Hazel does. She sends her friends away. She whispers in their ears, begs them to find another home, for the time being, watches them go.

Arthur hugs his daughter when the last sheep moves out of their sight. "Thank you, my daughter."

Hazel cannot say a word in return.

Arthur pulls away and looks at Mercy. "Now," he says. "You must make haste back through the portal. I shall be right behind you." He looks around the forest. "There might very well be eyes, returning at this precise moment."

The girls do as he bids them and disappear through the portal. Arthur takes a deep breath, sweeps his eyes once more across the forest that appears to be unchanged, but for the missing sheep, and follows them.

It is true that there is a man, a very young man, watching Arthur and the girls. Only he is not watching them so much as he is sleeping, for this young man stayed up far too late playing cards with his friends in a tent last eve. They made sure to remain as quiet as they could, with as little light as possible, for the captain did not like them staying up too late before an important day such as this one. And after all the traps had been hung throughout the forest, this man was, alas, the very one put in charge of the first watch in this exact part of the forest.

It is with great irony that we might remember what Captain Greyson tells his men on the eve before any momentous task. "Much has been missed because someone did not get enough sleep," he says.

Yes. It is true, for right here, before us, is a man who has folded his hands and rested, rather than keeping diligent watch over his part of the forest, and just what has he missed? Two children. A man. A portal, most important of all. The very things his fellow men have spent their days searching for, and this man missed it due to a nap. His fellow soldiers might have gone home for a good nights' sleep in their own beds, rather than continuing the search. They might have enjoyed a hot meal round their tables. They might have been set free.

But, you see, one man wanted for a nap.

Yet there is something.

Oh, yes. There is something.

Practice

Maude and Arthur began their lessons, and Maude proved to be a good student, quicker than Arthur even suspected. They continued meeting every evening, though both of them showed the signs of too little sleep and, if one knew what to look for, magic exhaustion in the coming weeks. While most villagers were curled comfortably in their beds, Maude and Arthur worked through every spell Arthur knew, ceasing only once they had reached their limit for the night (for magic always has a limit, you see, some expenditure on the magician's part that ensures he does not use it too often or too flippantly. Magic does not wish to be used for ill, though many magicians have used it for such. Those magicians often take to their beds for weeks after their great display, though the stories never tell this detail.). Maude and Arthur used their staffs, disguised as walking sticks, to help them back to the village, for they were nearly too tired to walk.

At times, they had so used everything within them that they considered sleeping on the banks of the river, but Arthur knew better than this. There were other secrets that could be discovered were they to do something so rash, for in his heart, Arthur was falling in love with Maude, and Maude with him.

Some nights they sat on the riverside, and instead of practicing magic, they talked. They talked of his travels, the sights he had seen, though Maude noticed that he never said much about his birthing place. She talked about her father, which led to talking of her mother.

"Your father is a skilled woodworker," Arthur said.

"He says the same of you," Maude said. "I have heard him in conversation with other men in the village."

"And he has treated you well, I suppose?" Arthur said.

"Well enough," Maude said. "Though not so well as when Mother lived."

"And your mother?" Arthur said. "You knew her?"

"For too little time," Maude said.

"You got your gift of magic from her," Arthur said.

"Yes," Maude said. "My mother was a Prophetess for a time. The king would bring her to his castle and give her great gifts to tell him what would happen in his future."

"What kind of future?" Arthur said.

Maude knew he was asking how far her mother could See. A prophet's power was measured by how far into the future they could See. "A month or two, so I have heard," she said. "I was too young to remember. I mostly remember the food." Arthur looked at her. "The king paid us in food. So our table was not so empty as it is now." She looked toward the waters, stilled in the silent night. "It was a different time, I suppose."

They were quiet for some minutes, and then Arthur said, "What happened to your mother?"

"She grew ill," she said. "A burning fever took her."

"And no one could heal it?" Arthur said. Maude heard something in his voice. She turned to him. His eyes were shadowed. Troubled.

"No," she said. "We do not have healers in White Wind."

"Every village has healers," Arthur said.

"Ours died of the same fever," Maude said.

Arthur was silent.

"What is it?" she said, for she could tell that there was something.

Arthur shook his head. "An oddity," he said. "Do you

not agree?"

Maude supposed it was. She said so. But Arthur did not say anything else, and so she let the wondering slide away.

"How old were you?" Arthur said after a time. "When your mother died?"

"A girl of seven," she said.

"Well," Arthur said. "Shall we begin tonight's lesson?"

"Yes, I suppose we shall," Maude said, for she did not steal from her house and risk Arthur's life to talk about her mother. They climbed to their feet, Arthur helping Maude wipe the grass from her skirt.

She loved him even more after that night.

And there were other nights as well. Nights when Arthur touched Maude's cheek for the briefest of moments, nights when she wondered if, perhaps, he had grown to love her as she had grown to love him. Nights when they lay beneath the hollow, a hole carved in the treetops where they could gaze at the stars, their hands touching at the fingertips. Nights when the magic did not matter so much as the presence.

They practiced for hours upon hours, every evening, treading back to their sleeping places only when the night had grown considerably darker and even the creatures of the forest did not stir, when all was silent and still around them. Arthur taught Maude more in a few hours than her grandmother had ever taught her in months of instruction, back before she had disappeared without a trace. Maude's magic, it seemed, merely needed an awakening. Arthur was a good teacher. He gave her magic the rest of what it needed, and soon, she was as skilled as he was.

Maude clung to his instruction as if, to her, it meant the difference between life and death.

And, perhaps, one day it would.

Shoe

The sun is hidden, so Prince Virgil does not know what hour it is when he wakes. It is dark, gray, cold in his chambers, as if light and warmth do not live in a world without children.

Why would it? The laughter of children is the light of a world. The presence of children grant warmth to even the coldest midnight.

Prince Virgil rises from his bed, pulls on his clothes, black pantaloons today, with a black tunic and a black cape. He wraps a royal robe around his shoulders, the only color he permits on a shadowed day like this one. It is soft, purple, rimmed in gold.

He steps out into the hallway. At least the torches are lit. The hallway shines bright compared to his chambers. He is glad for it. He has never liked this hallway, in truth. It is too long, with too many picture of the old kings who have ruled the kingdom. Many of them have kind eyes, but there are also the eyes of his grandfather. When he was a younger boy, he used to imagine that the eyes of these portraits followed him down this hall, and once, when he convinced himself to look back, he saw that it was true. Now he does not look at the portraits. In fact, he tries to ignore them.

Except that today, his grandfather's portrait stops him.

King Sebastien's painted likeness has cold blue eyes, the eyes of a hard man. Staring at his grandfather's portrait, painted in his younger days, Prince Virgil shivers. He did not know his grandfather. His father might be a hard man, but the eyes of his grandfather hold more cruelty, more hunger, more intelligence, perhaps. Not that Prince Virgil would ever call his father anything but intelligent, but the truth is, he did not have the wits of, say, Queen Clarion. Prince Virgil knows this. It is, perhaps, why King Willis is not such a frightening man as King Sebastien was in his time, though King Willis tries to be every now and again.

Prince Virgil moves to his father's portrait, struck by the difference between the young man on the wall and the man who sits in the throne room. His father had been a smaller man once, with eyes that shone with, what is it—hope?

Love? Mercy? Prince Virgil looks back at his grandfather, back to his father, back to his grandfather, again and again. His father's eyes were made for warmth. His grandfather's eyes were made for terror. And somewhere along the way, King Willis had become more like his father before him, though he was not so very cruel as all that. One might, perhaps, argue that imprisoning innocent children and hunting the rest of them down is, in fact, a very cruel thing to do, but Prince Virgil must consider what it is his father has not done with the children. He has not killed them, after all. Most of the people still have their lives, though there are many, both children and parents, missing. Looking at King Sebastien's portrait, he is not so certain that the same would be true were he still living.

Prince Virgil steps away from the portraits. One day his will hang beside his father's. When he is a man, when he is king. Unless the throne is no longer his…

Unless…

That would not happen. His father would not permit it to happen. He would, somehow, recover his magic, for even now, even after one hundred forty-three prophets have come bearing the same news—that Prince Virgil is a boy born without the gift of magic—our prince still holds hope that his is merely a dormant magic, that it will, one day, be recovered.

Poor, dear boy.

Prince Virgil hears a scuffle at the end of the hall. His mother is leaving her bedchambers, dressed in an elaborate gown of red and gold, with sleeves that join the hem of her dress. She turns to him and appears startled that he is there. "Virgil," she says. "I did not expect to meet you here." She smiles.

He smiles back. "I was on my way to join Father in the throne room."

Queen Clarion's smile falters. "Your father," she says. Her voice holds a stiffness he has not heard before. "Yes, of course. I shall not keep you."

Prince Virgil takes her arm. "Where are you going?" he says.

Queen Clarion glances toward the front doors. "I need a walk," she says. "Perhaps to the village." She does not say more. Prince Virgil wonders what she could possibly want to see in the village. The people no longer come out of their houses. He knows, for he has visited a few times. They did not even seem to notice him peering in the windows.

Prince Virgil and Queen Clarion make it to the castle entranceway, which is nearly as long as the hallway between the bedchambers and here. His mother turns toward the doors. He turns toward the throne room.

"Virgil," Queen Clarion says. He spins on his heel.

"Yes, Mother?" he says.

"Come see me after you are done with your father," Queen Clarion says. "Please."

Prince Virgil dips his head. Queen Clarion turns away. He strides toward the throne room doors.

"Oh, and Virgil?" his mother calls again. He turns to face her once more. "I visit the village for the people. They are very sad. It is the kind thing to do."

He watches her slip from the door, which closes behind her with a clack that echoes through the hall. He looks up at the marble ceiling, carved with its intricate designs. She has given him much to consider. But, perhaps, not so much as his father will give him, for when Prince Virgil opens the throne room doors, King Willis stands before a mirror Prince Virgil has never before seen. He wonders how he could have missed something so large and golden and… large. And then he sees the red velvet curtain that must have draped it. He has seen that, of course—an object concealed by a red velvet curtain. Never what was under it.

Prince Virgil moves closer, silent on his feet. King Willis appears to be talking to the mirror. And before Prince Virgil can register what it is, exactly, that he is seeing, his father turns, abruptly, nearly knocking the looking glass from its stand. "Virgil," he says. He bends to retrieve the velvet cover from the floor. "I did not expect you so soon." King Willis hastily throws the curtain over the looking glass.

"What is it, Father?" Prince Virgil says.

"This," King Willis says. He gestures toward the looking glass, covered once again. "This is only a silly old mirror."

"Were you speaking to the mirror?" Prince Virgil says. He cannot look his father full in the face, afraid of what his answer might be.

"Speaking," King Willis says. "Speaking to a mirror?" The king's face has grown quite red. And then, rather than contrive a story that does not make sense (for what story makes sense when we are hurrying it along?), King Willis says, "I speak to myself sometimes. I want to make sure I look stately." He straightens his shoulders.

It is just as Prince Virgil fears. He says nothing, however. He chooses to pretend his father never said the words at all.

"You will hold court with me today?" King Willis says.

Prince Virgil knows very well that there has been no holding court for quite some time, even before the children were taken from their families. The people of Fairendale, you see, did not respect the decisions of their king, so they began settling disputes on their own. Not that there were many disputes. But Prince Virgil knows that they took their decisions from Arthur, not his father.

Now Arthur is gone. So there can, perhaps, be people visiting the court, that is, if the people can bring themselves to venture from their homes.

King Willis looks at his son expectantly. "Yes, Father," Prince Virgil says, for he does not want to disappoint. He joins his father on the stage, and they turn toward the doors, where not a soul walks through. They remain in their expectant poses for quite some time before King Willis turns to his son and says, "Shall we break for our noonday meal?"

Prince Virgil has been eating the breads that King Willis keeps near his throne, so, in truth, he is not hungry at all. But he nods his head and follows his father to the great dining hall, where a feast will be laid at the flick of the king's wrist. It is as if, dear reader, our king possesses the gift of magic, though we know he does not. Prince Virgil watches. The slight movement. The servants running. The table stacked with roast and greens and a pie made from apples. Is this what it is like to be a king? Servants at your beck and call? Prince Virgil has never wanted for anything, but this, this flicking a wrist and seeing what you desire laid out before you, this is too wonderful to lose. Prince Virgil's grip on the throne clenches a bit tighter. His father, you see, knows precisely what will sway the prince, for this is the secret of the golden throne. It knows precisely what those who sit on it most desire. Or, rather, King Willis has been told. And now he works this telling into his every move.

This is why, after Prince Virgil has heaped his plate high of the rich food so different from what he has been fed thus far, eating in the less formal, less royal hall where his father did not dine, King Willis opens his mouth with, perhaps, a larger bite of roast in it than might, in others' estimation, leave room for polite conversation and says, "Your uncle."

Two simple words, but they pull Prince Virgil's eyes to his father's face, shining even in the day's low light. King Willis puts down his fork. "Your mother does not know of what she speaks."

His mother? His uncle? What is it his father would like to tell him? Prince Virgil prefers a silent dinner to this wondering one.

"Your uncle was a foolish man," King Willis says.

Prince Virgil takes a bite of a roll, as inconspicuously as

he might. It is, you see, too wonderful to leave on a plate so it cools. He does not say a word, for Prince Virgil knows better than to talk with food in his mouth. He mostly dines with his mother, you see, and mothers are good for teaching manners. But his father does not desire an answer, for he is accustomed to delivering his monologues without a single word spoken from anyone else in the room who may have the very great privilege of hearing their king's mindless chatter. Oh, for sure, not everything out of the king's mouth is mindless chatter. There are nuggets, of course. But King Willis, now, talks and talks and talks about the foolishness of his brother, the true and rightful king, though he would never admit that title aloud. His brother did not deserve the throne, though he was the one born with magic. His brother made his choice and must now live with it.

"He would not have made a good king," King Willis says. He wipes his mouth with a blue napkin and places it on the table, as if he is finished. But a man like King Willis is hardly ever finished with eating.

His words bother Prince Virgil, for there is still so much of the old prince that has not yet been touched by his father and the golden glory of a throne. "How do you know?" he says.

King Willis tilts his head. His eyes rake his son's face. He does not like to be contradicted, you see, especially from a boy. "What is it you say?"

Prince Virgil realizes, then, that it might have been more prudent to close his mouth. Was that not what all the sages wrote in their volumes of proverbs? A man with many words is a man deemed foolish. A man who speaks without thinking may as well wear a fool's cap.

The boy clears his throat. "Nothing, Father," he says, for he hopes his father did not hear him at all.

But King Willis, though he is not a great listener, is a skilled listener. He listens to the mumblings of servants. He listens to the talk of the village, through his trusty spy, who flits about the town, landing on windowsills and collecting the conversation within. The spy has not been needed for some time, for the people do not seem to move from their homes.

The king has, alas, heard the words of his son. "How do I know?" he says.

Prince Virgil drops his head. He may as well wear the fool's cap for a moment. "How do you know he would not have been a good king if he never sat the throne?"

The silence between them is worse than the speaking. Prince Virgil much prefers the chatter. The quiet steals across him like a cold breath of fear.

King Willis does not rise. He does not strike the table. He does not breathe, one might think, for it is obvious when King Willis breathes. The very buttons on his shirt tremble. But the king must be in good humor this afternoon, for when he speaks, his voice smoothes calm across the whipped waters. "I know," he says, "because he was just like my grandfather. Weak." He leans back in his chair, threads his hands together. "It takes a strong man to lead a kingdom. Especially one as desired as Fairendale." He stares at his son. Prince Virgil tries not to look away from his black, beady eyes. "Are you a strong man, son?"

He does not know the answer to his father's question. Is he strong? Is it a strong man who would give away the secret of his friend for the safety of the village children? Is it a strong man who stands by while his father destroys the village and all the people he loved anyway? Is it a strong man who sits in a warm castle while village children sit in the dark dungeons below the dungeons, kept alive only by bread and water?

Well, you see why it is such a difficult question to answer. Strong, yes. Weak, yes. He is both.

Prince Virgil turns it over and over in his mind. Is his father a strong man? What does it mean to be strong? Does it mean cruelty? Does it mean kindness? Is it stronger to be cruel or to be kind?

King Willis answers for his son. "I think you are a strong man," he says. He stands from his chair with great difficulty, peeling layers of his belly from the sides of it. "Come now. Let us return to the throne room. Perhaps we shall have some news today. I feel change afoot."

So Prince Virgil follows his father through the wide double doors and back into the room that does not bear light as it once did. He watches the window as he walks to the platform where his father's throne waits. The sky has grown increasingly darker, though it is day. The gray reaches into his heart. He has a bad feeling about this day. He does not want to be here, in this room, for whatever may come. He suspects there will be news, but it is not the kind of news he will want to hear. So while he is concocting his reasons for leaving court early—extra studies, perhaps, though it is not an instruction day—his father arranges himself in the golden chair.

Prince Virgil remains, in the end. For a king must be strong, and he will one day be king. He will have to find his strength.

As we all must.

The sleeping soldier wakes. He looks around. He takes in the missing traps, the tracks of an animal that is more tame than wild, and there, a footprint. A single footprint that Arthur did not think to wipe away, for when fear beats a heart, a mind can forget the most important parts.

Someone has been here. And this soldier has missed it. He drops to his knees, examines the footprint, examines the tracks—sheep, he thinks—pats the grass all around. He crawls, searching the ground, searching for a clue, for there must be something here. Something left behind besides this most universal footprint that tells him nothing, only that someone was wearing shoes. To whose foot does it belong? How can he explain what he has found when there is no actual person in his possession? What might the captain do? The captain is a merciful man, to be sure, but this soldier fell asleep on his shift and missed the very ones that could have sent them all home.

The soldier sits back, drops his head to his chest. He should not have stayed up playing cards. That much is certain. He will never do it again.

His hand moves to his eyes, rubbing them. He is still so very tired. So he lies down, on his back, but something pierces between his shoulder blades. Something tiny. Something hard. Something left behind. He rises, turns, and leans ever closer to the grass, and finally he sees it, what looks like a tiny shoe. Is his exhausted mind playing tricks on him? Does it mean a thing at all? Could it belong to the missing children, or just another enchanted being of this haunted forest? He does not know. But he does pick it up, for this is enough news. This is enough discovery. This is enough hope. Or so he hopes.

He clutches the tiny shoe in his hand so he does not misplace it in his haste and runs as fast as his legs will carry him, back to the captain.

Escape

It has been said that all good things, alas, speed toward their endings. And because this, the learning of magic, the practicing of magic, the love between a teacher and his pupil, was, indeed, a very good thing, one might suppose that it is only natural for this good thing to end (though no one likes an ending, dear reader. Perhaps endings are unappreciated because they bring with them the unknown, as is certainly the case in our story.).

Maude's father came home one evening, so angry she could see the sweat forming on his brow and above his lip, even through the splatter of black hair growing there. She had seen this anger before. Sometimes, you see, the wine was too great for her father. He walked in through the door and promptly stumbled and fell. Maude caught him. "You," he said. That one word was so full of contempt and revulsion that Maude nearly dropped him. She had never heard her father speak in such a way, but, as they say, there is a first time for everything. (Beginnings and endings are very much the same, are they not? Bringing with them a great unknown.)

"Father," she said, for whatever her father had done in the past (and he was, for the most part, an honorable man), she could not bear to be the brunt of his anger.

"You!" he roared again, and he pushed her away. "Get your hands off me." She stumbled, her head smacking against the dining table. He pointed a finger at her, a fat finger that she had not noticed had even gotten fat. Had she been so consumed with Arthur and magic that she had not noticed how her father's bulk had changed? "You dare soil our name?"

What was he saying? What did he know?

"Father?" she said. "I do not understand."

She tried to see her father in her father, but she could not. She could see only a great, hulking mass standing before her and the door. For the first time in all her nineteen years, she felt afraid of him.

"You and that boy," he said. His voice broke in the middle of it. His words slurred together, one into another. "Bringing a curse on me and your mother!" His face had turned purple in his effort to form the words.

"It is not what you think, Father," she said. Her mind whirled. How did the villagers know? What was it they had told him? Where was Arthur?

The thought of Arthur squeezed her throat. Was he safe? Was he waiting? Could she summon him?

"Not what I think," her father said. His voice shook the walls. Everyone in the village could likely hear him, shouting as he was. Her insides burned. She must get away. She must get away now. And then he said the very words she dreaded hearing all along. "I know more than you think." His eyes gleamed in the firelight. "Magic." He growled the word, as if there was something evil in magic, as if her mother had not carried magic before she was born, as if he had never loved a person with the gift. The thought of it stole Maude's breath and blurred her eyes. Her father. He was her father, you see. A daughter longs for nearly nothing as she longs for a father's love.

"No," Maude said. "No, you are wrong." But her voice was weak, jagged, too unconvincing.

"He shall die!" her father shouted. "He shall be executed!" He leaned in, and she could smell the sour wine on his breath, even at this distance.

"No," she said. "Father, please!" She could not bear it

any longer. She moved toward the door, but her father threw her back. This time her head cracked a wall, and she saw black for a moment but grasped desperately at the light. By the time her vision cleared, her father loomed right above her. She rolled away quickly, upsetting his balance, and he stumbled just enough for her to reach the door. She slipped out silently, racing up the lane. She could see people gathered in the streets, their torches blazing. She could not let them reach Arthur first. She headed the back way to his rooms, but the people spotted her. They set chase.

She was sure they would catch her, but fear makes feet fast, and when she reached the doors of the inn, Arthur came bursting out. They fell into each other's arms, but he moved aside, too quickly, roughly grasping her hand. He drew her into the shadows and held her close for a moment more.

"I am sorry," he said. "I will have to leave."

"Take me with you," she said against his chest. "Please."

He pulled away so he could look into her eyes. He shook his head, and she could not bear it. She looked away. "No," he said. "No, I cannot. The wandering life I live is not fit for a woman as fine as you."

"A woman as fine as me," she said. "Look at me! I am no fine woman." And it was true that her skirts were torn in the escape from her drunken father, and her face held smudges of dirt from the fall to the floor. Her hair was sticky with what she supposed was blood.

"I must go," Arthur said. "If I want to live."

"They will kill me as well," Maude said. "When you are gone. You must take me with you."

"You will be safe," he said. "They would not dare hurt a woman."

"I would not live anyway," Maude said, but she said nothing more, for she did not want to tell him what was truly in her heart. But Arthur knew. He drew back and looked in her eyes so tenderly her nose burned with tears.

"My dear Maude," he said. "I must go."

"Please," she said. "Please. I will not be a burden."

His eyes softened again. "You would never be a burden," he said. "It is your safety I am concerned for."

"Then let me go!" she said. "My father is not well. The people…" She let the words hang between them. He pulled her to him again. She felt his gasp of a breath, the tightening of his arms.

"As you wish," he said, so softly she could hardly hear. "We will go together. But you must do everything I say."

He released her then, and she could see his face as he looked behind her. It flickered as if there were a light. She knew what she would find before she even turned around. The townspeople stood before them with torches turning their faces into grotesque masks, as if the night had brought out the worst monsters of all. And perhaps it had, for there is no more disturbing sight than man killing man. These men were out for blood.

Maude closed her eyes. They were too late. She had killed this man she loved. And perhaps they would let her live but she would not, in fact, live. Not without Arthur. When she opened her eyes, the people were still there, though she had, in truth, hoped they would not be. There were so many of them. So few of her and Arthur. They would not be able to explain.

"Magic man," one of the men said. He jabbed a torch in Arthur's direction. "This is why you have come."

Arthur did not say anything. He merely squeezed Maude's hand. "Magic," he said, and then the whole world shimmered before her. Flames leapt in the air and at their feet and all around them, dancing to a song they could not hear, touching no one. The people turned to one another, confused, unsure how the flames they had held moments ago now danced upon the air or before them on the ground and not one of them, nothing, in fact, burned, though the answer, of course, could be found in the very word Arthur said. The village men stared and turned and tried to catch their lights, bring them back where they belonged so the world made sense again, but no one could figure out how. They turned to Arthur, but there was no Arthur.

In all the confusion, Maude and Arthur had slipped away.

They waited to laugh until they had reached the deepest center of the forest, where no one dared venture in the dead of night. That was the very place Arthur turned Maude toward him and kissed her for the first time.

Trapped

Inside the underground house, there is the sound of an entire world breaking, shattering, falling down around them, though the house remains as it was. It startles the children, so a few of them scream and are hushed by their peers.

Hazel looks at her father, but her father only has eyes for her mother. They are large eyes, concerned eyes, terrified eyes. "What does it mean, Father?" Hazel has never considered that anything might go wrong with their plan, that this one, which appeared so safe at first glance, might very well have held danger. Every decision in life, you see, holds a little danger. We all risk at all times. Hazel has not yet learned this, but she is learning now.

"The portal," Arthur says. He stares at Maude, still. She stares at him, still. "The way out has been broken."

The children gasp and pitch their questions, "But how?" "What will we do?" "Will we die?" but Maude and Arthur are in no state to answer any of them.

"We are buried alive," Maude says, so softly the children almost do not hear over their own questions cracking the quiet. She falls into Arthur's arms with a silent weeping so loud it is deafening.

The children dare not say a word.

Don't miss out on the next Fairendale adventure!

How will the children escape the broken portal? Find out in Book 3: *The Perilous Crossing*.

The Established Order of the King's Guard
The Kingdom of Fairendale

Purpose

To protect the king and the royal family to the utmost of their ability, and, when that duty has been fulfilled, to protect the people of the land.

Eligibility

Any able-bodied man in the land can serve on the king's guard, even if he is a family man. If he is a family man, he must understand that the king's decrees come first, even if they negatively affect his family.

Hierarchy

The king's guard is comprised of any number of men. The current king of Fairendale has 210 men, including an honorable captain and a second-in-command. The king appoints both of these positions, on recommendation from officers or simply on his own whim.

Sir Greyson is the current captain of the king's guard in Fairendale. Sir Merrick is his second-in-command.

Benefits

A member of the king's guard will be given all the food, drink, clothes, housing, medicine, and other necessary living supplies that his family might require, for as long as he serves the king.

If a member of the king's guard is discharged honorably (which can happen if he has grown too old for service, as deemed by the king), he will continue to glean those benefits until he dies. If he is discharged dishonorably (which is subject to the king's interpretation) or dies in an inappropriate way (which is also subject to the king's interpretation), his family will no longer receive the benefits of service.

The kingdom will pay for all travel costs and food and shelter requirements during the travel of a member of the king's guard, while in the service to the king.

If a member of the king's guard defies the king by disobeying, betraying, or dishonoring his king, he will be dishonorably discharged from the king's guard and slain in whatever fashion the king requires. The king is also given leave to slay the member's entire family, including grandmothers, grandfathers, mother, father, sisters, brothers, spouse, children, and even aunts, uncles, and cousins, if he so desires.

Requirements

A member of the king's guard must conduct his business in an honorable way at all times, knowing that he is carrying both the reputation and the fate of the kingdom on his shoulders.

A member of the king's guard will faithfully serve his king, even when the king is apparently and obviously wrong. He must never question his king's ways, only follow them faithfully.

A member of the king's guard must never hesitate—a word that is here defined as pausing for more than three seconds—to follow through on an order.

A member of the king's guard must uphold all the laws of the king, even those that have not yet been signed into law.

A member of the king's guard will not live in the castle but in tents on the castle lawn, when he is not traveling.

A member of the king's guard agrees, upon knighthood, to leave his family for such a time as the king requires his service. He is only given leave when the king permits. If he permits.

A member of the king's guard will not dishonor his king by speaking ill of him, especially when outside the king's presence.

A member of the king's guard must always keep his wits about him, his sword sharp, and his armor and dress impeccably clean.

Initiation

A member of the king's guard is inducted into the guard by way of knighthood. The probational member must kneel before the king, bow his head, and agree upon all the requirements, after which the captain of the king's guard will knight him and present to him a sword procured from the ancient sword room of Fairendale castle.

The member's family can be present at the time of

initiation, after which they are invited to enjoy a sweet roll and a glass or two of lemon water.

How to Live Sustainably in Fairendale

By Garron of Fairendale
Head Gardener

The countryside around Fairendale is abundant with green grasses and plants by the hundreds, but if you do not know these plants, you will find yourself charmed in the worst of ways. Some of the plants in the fields surrounding Fairendale will make you fall asleep simply by smelling them, and so we, the people of Fairendale, warn our children to keep away from the green open fields, particularly those closest to the Weeping Woods. The grasses will sometimes allow a traveler to pass unaffected, but many times they will not.

This, as you might imagine, limits the sustainability, which is simply a fancy word for how people live, of Fairendale. With such large green fields, one would think we could raise animals or plant enormous gardens, but that is not the case.

Fortunately, we do have a safe patch of land where I have cultivated a large and beautiful garden. This garden feeds the people of Fairendale. It feeds, too, the sheep of Fairendale, which is the only animal we have found that is immune to the charm of the grasses. I believe that we do not need these sheep as much as the villagers claim we do, for a garden provides enough sustenance to live on, but that is a story for another day.

Here are the top three things you will need to sustain yourself in a land like Fairendale:

1. A robust garden.

All you need for a robust garden is a plot of land you can cultivate. I found this plot of land on the easternmost side of Fairendale. To begin this garden, I asked Arthur of Fairendale to build me large rectangles made of wood. I then turned some soil in the field beyond (alas, I fell asleep twice) and used that soil to fill the rectangles, plunging seeds deep within the bed and watering regularly. In a matter of time, I had a garden.

The weather in Fairendale is quite mild, which means that we can grow all manner of tasty food—tomatoes, cucumbers, carrots, and many other delicious vegetables, as well as strawberries and blackberries and grapes (these latter fruits are grown on wooden trellises, also supplied by Arthur), and the base of all our sustenance: wheat.

I am very proud of my garden.

2. A dedication to weeding the garden.

Every fruitful garden must be diligently weeded. The children of Fairendale occasionally help me, but mostly I use the daughter of my assistant, whose name is Ruby. She is quite good at what she does, and I do not have to explain to her the difference between a weed and a plant.

3. A healthy herb garden.

Herbs are not only good for seasoning the dishes we are able to cook in Fairendale, but they are also quite good for healing people. The village healer uses my herbs regularly.

They include basil, chamomile, echinacea, feverfew, lavender, lemon balm, marigold, parsley, peppermint, rosemary, sage, thyme, and St. John's Wort.

The people of Fairendale use these for a variety of things, including:

Flatulence

Cuts and scrapes

Head aches

Stomach aches

Colds

Relaxation

Sleeping draughts

Wounds

Digestive problems

Bad breath

Concentration

Throat aches

As you can see, it is possible to live on very little, if one is diligent about maintaining and cultivating a robust garden.

The Royal Family of Fairendale

King Willis: The current king of Fairendale. Has a deep love for sweet rolls, and it shows in his, well, wideness.

Queen Clarion: The current queen of Fairendale. Is underestimated by her husband, but we shall see just how powerful she is soon enough.

Prince Virgil: Son of King Willis and Queen Clarion, best friend of Theo. Prefers rye bread with melted butter to sweet rolls, depending on the day.

King Sebastien: Deceased king of Fairendale, exception to the line of boys who tried to steal thrones and were, upon failing at their quest, forever banished to sail the Violet Sea. Was killed by a blackbird.

The Villagers of Fairendale

Arthur: Village furniture maker and magic instructor to girls who possess the gift of magic. Is a bit reckless but always manages to come out on the other side—though one is not always assured it will be so.

Maude: Arthur's wife. Bakes spectacular pumpkin sugar cookies. Prefers caution to reckless abandon.

Hazel: Daughter of Arthur and Maude, twin of Theo. Cares for the village sheep and can even, amazingly, understand them.

Theo: Son of Arthur and Maude, twin of Hazel. Finishes his chores early so he can sit in on magic lessons.

Mercy: Daughter of Cora, best friend of Hazel. Prefers spectacular acts of magic to "boring" ones.

Cora: Mother of Mercy, widow, shape shifter. A woman who moves.

Garron: The town gardener. Talks to plants as though they can hear him. Has three sons: 12-year-old twins and a 13-year-old.

Bertie: The town baker. Enjoys showing off his air-kneading skills for the children.

Staff of Fairendale Castle

Garth: Page for King Willis, the oldest of twelve children. Sometimes calls King Willis "Your Wideness."

Cook: One of the few shape shifters in the land. Shape shifts into a bear. Is highly annoyed by her assistant, Calvin.

Calvin: An orphan who began working as Cook's assistant instead of traveling to live with distant relatives in Ashvale—and so did not perish in the Fire Mountain that claimed the entire population of Ashvale many years ago. Tasked with feeding the prisoners in the dungeons beneath the dungeons.

Sir Greyson: Captain of the king's guard. Receives

medicine, which keeps his mother alive, in exchange for his service to the king. Carries a magical sword that cannot be lifted by any but him.

Sir Merrick: Second in command to Sir Greyson.

Important Prophets

Aleen: A prophetess who is one hundred forty-two years old, from the kingdom of White Wind. Wears ebony skin and what appears to be a collection of snakes for hair (though it is not).

Yerin: A prophet who is one hundred forty-two years old, from the wild woodland between Lincastle and Eastermoor. Has white hair that makes the dark of the dungeons where he is imprisoned a bit less dark.

Dragons of Morad

Zorag: King of the dragons of Morad. Lost his parents in the Great Battle, when King Sebastien stole the throne from the Good King Brendon. Would like nothing more than peace.

Blindell: Zorag's cousin, raised as the dragon king's son. Lost his parents in the Great Battle, when King Sebastien stole the throne from the Good King Brendon. Would like nothing more than revenge.

Larus: One of the elder dragons of Morad, male. Counselor to Zorag.

Malera: One of the elder dragons of Morad, female. Counselor to Zorag.

The lost 12-year-old children of Fairendale

Ursula

Chester

Charles

Thumbelina (known as Lina among the children)

Minnie

Jasper

Frederick

Ruby

Martin

Oscar

Homer

Anna

Aurora

Rose

Edgar

Harriet (known as Hattie among the children)

Isabel (known as Izzy among the children)

Ralph

Dorothy
Julian
Tom Thumb
Philip

About the Author

While she has never possessed the gift of magic, L.R.'s teachers claimed she had a gift for words, which one might agree is quite like a gift of magic. Bringing a story to life that did not exist before is very much like transforming an old shoe into a dish towel. L.R. feels quite honored that she was given this gift and hopes to use it to encourage other young writers to discover their own gifts, for what is the world without words and stories?

L.R. is the queen of her castle in San Antonio, TX. She lives with her king and her six young princes, who daily give her inspiration for more grand tales of magic and adventure.

www.lrpatton.com

A Note From L.R.

I hope you've enjoyed reading this book from the annals of Fairendale's history. The world of Fairendale has been a lovely world to create, and I've had fun sketching maps, re-reading fairy tales and thinking, endlessly, about characters and their plights—because a series like this one takes lots and lots of time and hard work. But because it's always been my dream to create a fantasy world and share it with my readers, I knew it was something I had to do. (So, you see, dreams really do come true.)

If you have any questions about Fairendale or simply want to send me a note to tell me who your favorite character is or what kinds of extras you'd like to see me release in the future (a *Creatures of the Violet Sea* is coming soon!), email me at lr@lrpatton.com. I always enjoy hearing from my young readers.

Please consider leaving (or ask your parent to leave) a review of this book wherever you bought it. Reviews help get books into the hands of potential new readers, which is incredibly important for authors like me. And don't forget to pick up your free bonus materials when you stop by my web site! (www.lrpatton.com)

Thank you so much for supporting my work.

In love,

L.R.

Enjoy more stories from the magical Fairendale series:

LRPatton.com/Fairendale

Starter Library

Once upon a time...

The kingdom of Fairendale used to be the most peaceful in all the lands. Its people had never held a weapon before. And now they must, for the sake of the land. For the sake of their families. For the sake of their beloved king.

Read all about the king who had no heir, the girl who had magic, the dragon they loved, and the battle that changed everything in Fairendale's short story prequel, "The Good King's Fall."

Get it FREE, along with bonus materials "The Magical Rules of Fairendale" and "The Lands of Fairendale," for a limited time.

To get your FREE bonus materials, visit *
LRPatton.com/goodking

*Must be 13 or older to be eligible